R. A. Spratt

FRIDAY BARNES
Danger Ahead

PUFFIN BOOKS

PUFFIN BOOKS

UK | USA | Canada | Ireland | Australia
India | New Zealand | South Africa | China

Penguin Random House Australia is part of the Penguin Random House group of
companies whose addresses can be found at global.penguinrandomhouse.com.

First published by Random House Australia in 2017
This edition published by Puffin Books, an imprint of
Penguin Random House Australia Pty Ltd, in 2020

Cover illustration by Lilly Piri, www.littlegalaxie.com
Cover design by Kirby Armstrong © Penguin Random House Australia Pty Ltd
Internal design and typesetting by Midland Typesetters, Australia

Printed and bound in Australia by Griffin Press, an accredited ISO AS/NZS 14001
Environmental Management Systems printer

 A catalogue record for this
book is available from the
National Library of Australia

ISBN 978 1 76 089216 6 (Paperback)

Penguin Random House Australia uses papers that are natural and recyclable
products, made from wood grown in sustainable forests. The logging and
manufacture processes are expected to conform to the environmental
regulations of the country of origin.

penguin.com.au

To James

Chapter 1

Parting

'I guess this is goodbye,' said Friday.

She and her best friend, Melanie, were standing on the school driveway with Ian Wainscott. Ian had a fully packed backpack sitting at his feet. It wasn't a large backpack because Ian was heading off to the Cayman Islands, where the average temperature was a balmy thirty degrees and he wouldn't need an extensive wardrobe.

'I guess,' agreed Ian.

'After nearly a whole year of romantic banter, that's the best you two can come up with?' asked Melanie.

Ian rolled his eyes.

Friday stared at her own feet. She was starting to feel emotions, which always made her uncomfortable. She looked up at Ian's face.

'Be careful,' said Friday.

'That's better,' said Melanie approvingly.

'The Cayman Islands has its own species of alligator,' continued Friday. 'And while it isn't large enough to cause fatal injuries, it has been known to amputate limbs of incautious swimmers.'

Melanie shook her head sadly. 'You may never see Ian again, and all you can think to say is to warn him not to get bitten by an obscure species of alligator?'

'If I didn't mention it and he did get bitten, who'd be foolish then?' snapped Friday.

'You,' said Melanie. 'Still you.'

At the far end of the driveway, a black car turned in through the school gates.

'This must be my ride,' said Ian.

'Look . . .' said Friday, searching her enormous brain for some suitable words. Something that would encapsulate all that she felt and all that she had been through with this distractingly handsome boy. 'I guess I should say . . .'

Ian interrupted her. 'Forget it, Barnes. You're terrible at this stuff.'

Friday then entirely forgot whatever thoughts she had, because Ian took her by surprise when he wrapped her in a big hug. For one long second she felt warm and squeezed. He smelled of boy, which wasn't as repellent as she had thought. Then he let go.

Melanie was crying. 'This is better than any Mexican soap opera our housekeeper Marta ever forced me to watch.'

The black car pulled up alongside them. It was so sleek and new, that they had barely heard the purring powerful motor as it approached. A dapper middle-aged driver got out and came around to pick up Ian's bag.

'Your father must be doing well to afford all this,' said Friday.

'Dad has a knack for landing on his feet,' said Ian, 'then rubbing everyone's noses in it.'

The driver held open the car door and Ian disappeared inside. The windows were tinted, so Friday couldn't see Ian anymore as the driver efficiently shut the door, put the backpack in the boot and slid into the driver's seat.

The car pulled away and crackled over the gravel down to the main road. Friday and Melanie watched it disappear into the stream of traffic.

'I'm sure we'll see him again,' said Melanie.

'Yes,' agreed Friday.

'He is extremely good-looking,' remarked Melanie. 'If nothing else, Ian will be all over the gossip magazines in a couple of years when he is old enough to be a jetsetting playboy.'

Friday just nodded. She didn't want to speak. There was a huge lump in her throat. And she suspected any attempt to move her face would cause her to burst into tears.

'Things are going to be very different here at Highcrest without him,' said Melanie. 'Maybe it's time for you to move on and start irritating other boys.'

Chapter 2

Terrible Mistake

The rest of the day was fairly quiet. Melanie wasn't much of a chatterbox at the best of times, largely because she was usually asleep. But Friday was quiet too, because she was lost in her own thoughts that were, for once, about something other than science. The two girls were wandering back across the sports fields after their last class of the day.

Mr Fontana, the PE teacher, had been trying to force them to play hockey. In the end he had sent them to the sin bin for the duration of the lesson – Melanie, because she'd shrieked any time someone hit a ball near her, and Friday, because she'd been scaring the other players by telling them the exact force a hockey ball had as it shot through the air at sixty kilometres an hour, and how much damage that could do to the bones in your face.

'Isn't that your Uncle Bernie's car?' asked Melanie.

Friday looked up. There was a dark plume of smoke progressing up the school driveway, with a beaten-up old brown jalopy at the centre of it.

'What's he doing here?' wondered Friday.

'Perhaps he needs help with a case,' said Melanie.

'Let's find out,' said Friday as she changed course and started towards the visitors car park.

'Friday!' cried Uncle Bernie as he got out of the car. 'I almost didn't recognise you in a gym skirt.'

'I almost didn't recognise you,' said Friday. 'Are you wearing a new suit?'

Uncle Bernie looked unusually smart in a well-cut suit, with a clean shirt and tie. Even his hair was neatly cut.

Uncle Bernie blushed. Another car door slammed. Ian's mother emerged from the passenger side of the car.

'Mrs Wainscott!' exclaimed Friday.

'You look lovely too,' noticed Melanie.

Mrs Wainscott usually only wore filthy gardening clothes, and hair that looked like it hadn't been combed for a week. But today she was wearing a lovely yellow dress and her hair was styled nicely. It even looked like she had used hairspray.

'Are you two going somewhere?' asked Friday.

'Oh my gosh!' exclaimed Melanie. 'Rings!'

'What?' asked Friday. When Melanie said 'rings', her mind immediately thought of Wagner's Ring Cycle of operas.

'They're wearing rings!' exclaimed Melanie before turning to Uncle Bernie. 'You're married, aren't you?!' She leapt forward and gave him a big hug. He was blushing as red as a beetroot now.

Melanie let go and ran around the car to hug Mrs Wainscott as well.

'Is this true?' asked Friday.

Uncle Bernie nodded. 'Helena and I have just been to the registry office, where she did me the honour of becoming my wife.'

'Congratulations,' said Friday, giving her uncle an awkward hug. 'I'm so happy you've found someone.'

'So am I,' said Uncle Bernie.

'You know, statistically, married men live longer,' said Friday.

'I've heard that,' agreed Uncle Bernie.

'Especially if they marry avid gardeners who force them to eat lots of vegetables,' said Friday with a smile.

Uncle Bernie grinned. 'Not *too many* vegetables.'

'You've got the pizza place on speed dial, haven't you?' said Friday.

Uncle Bernie shook his head. He checked over his shoulder to see Melanie admiring Mrs Wainscott's, or rather Mrs Barnes', wedding ring. Uncle Bernie showed Friday his smartphone. 'I've got the app. I just wait until she's out in the backyard with her veggies and hit send on my order.'

'So long as you're happy,' said Friday.

'Are you here to take Friday to your reception?' asked Melanie, calling over the car.

'Well, yes,' said Uncle Bernie. 'And Ian.'

Uncle Bernie and Mrs Wainscott looked at each other and smiled.

Friday looked at them and frowned. 'But he's not here,' she said.

'Is he away on some excursion or something?' asked Uncle Bernie. 'I know he's not off on camp yet. That's not for another two weeks.'

Friday glanced at Melanie to see if she would be of any support. Melanie just looked amazed at the situation and was clearly not intending to volunteer any information.

'Ian left this morning for the Cayman Islands,' said Friday. 'Didn't you know?'

'What?!' cried Mrs Wainscott.

'His father sent him a package with airline tickets, a passport and money so Ian could go and visit him,' said Friday.

'But he can't just leave the country!' exclaimed Mrs Wainscott. 'I have custody of him.'

'I wouldn't take offence,' said Melanie. 'Ian probably just forgot. When you're away on your own at boarding school, you do forget that technically your parents are in charge of you.'

'Are you saying I don't adequately supervise my son?' demanded Mrs Wainscott.

Uncle Bernie stared at his feet. Friday watched Melanie, anxious to see what she might say.

'I don't want to be rude to you at this emotional time,' said Melanie kindly, 'so I'm going to smile and not say anything.' Melanie smiled, which amazingly did seem to placate Mrs Wainscott infinitesimally.

'We'd better speak to the Headmaster and get to the bottom of this,' said Uncle Bernie.

'Poor Headmaster,' said Melanie. 'He hates it when students abscond. Especially so early in the morning.'

Chapter 3

Thin Air

'He did what?!' exclaimed the Headmaster.

'He went to the Cayman Islands,' said Friday.

Friday, Melanie, Uncle Bernie and Mrs Wainscott had all gathered in the Headmaster's office and were trying to explain the situation.

'And you didn't think to mention it to me?' demanded the Headmaster.

'We assumed he told you himself,' protested Friday.

'Actually, I didn't,' volunteered Melanie, 'but only because I didn't think about it at all.'

'Well, let me make it clear for you,' said the Headmaster sarcastically. 'Students are not allowed to take off to tropical resorts in the middle of an academic term.'

'Is that a school rule?' asked Friday.

The Headmaster looked like he wanted to leap across his desk and strangle her. 'Yes! Yes, it is!' he said. 'I'm going to write it into the rule book today and backdate it so that when Ian does come back I can throw him out again.'

'He just went to visit his dad,' argued Friday.

'But his father doesn't have custody!' wailed Mrs Wainscott.

'We'd better ring Roger and find out what's going on,' said Uncle Bernie.

'Who?' asked Melanie.

'Roger is Mr Wainscott's name,' said Friday.

'Really?' said Melanie. 'How funny. I wish I'd known that before. I would have giggled more when I saw him.'

'What's his phone number?' Uncle Bernie asked the Headmaster.

'I don't know,' said the Headmaster.

'Don't you have it on file?' asked Uncle Bernie.

'It's the responsibility of the parent who has custody to keep the personal details we have on file updated,' said the Headmaster.

Everyone looked at Mrs Wainscott.

'I don't have his number,' said Mrs Wainscott. 'He never used to give me his phone number, even when we were married. He said he didn't want to tie up the line in case an important business call came through. So he's hardly going to start now.'

'Then how do we get hold of the man?' asked the Headmaster.

'You could ring the Cayman Islands directory enquiries,' said Friday. 'But given that the entire country is a haven for tax exiles, I'm guessing the vast majority of the population don't have listed phone numbers.'

'My boy is lost!' wept Mrs Wainscott. 'Lost forever!' She collapsed on Uncle Bernie, sobbing.

'This isn't turning out to be much of a wedding day for you, is it?' said Melanie sympathetically.

Suddenly the door burst open as Miss Priddock, the school secretary, ran in crying. She went straight to the Headmaster and collapsed, sobbing on him.

The Headmaster looked thoroughly uncomfortable with the situation. 'My dear, get a hold of yourself. This is no way to behave in the workplace.'

'But there's a dreadful man on the telephone,' said Miss Priddock between sobs. 'He's yelling at me using the most abusive language.'

'Is it one of your boyfriends?' asked Melanie. Miss Priddock was very attractive. She had rather a lot of boyfriends or, to be fair, men who wanted to be her boyfriend.

'It's a parent,' sniffed Miss Priddock. 'I told him the Headmaster was busy in a meeting and he said things that were very rude, and I'm fairly sure anatomically impossible.'

'Which parent is threatening us now?' sighed the Headmaster.

'Roger Wainscott,' said Miss Priddock.

'Then put him through immediately!' yelled the Headmaster. 'Have you no common sense?'

Miss Priddock burst into even louder tears and ran out of the office back to her desk.

'Do you think she's going to put the call through?' Uncle Bernie whispered to Friday.

'If she knows how to,' said Friday. 'Miss Priddock is not the most wildly competent secretary.'

They all flinched when the phone on the Headmaster's desk started ringing. The Headmaster took a deep breath, braced himself and picked up the phone. 'Mr Wainscott . . . ?' He then held the phone a foot away from his head because Mr Wainscott was yelling at him so loudly it could have given him long-term hearing damage. Mr Wainscott used very rude language, but the gist of what he had to say was that he was very angry and he thought the Headmaster was not good at his job.

'Your wife, I mean, ex-wife, and her partner –' began the Headmaster.

'*Husband*,' corrected Uncle Bernie proudly.

'Congratulations!' said the Headmaster, before remembering he was talking on the phone. 'Where was I? Yes, they're here along with two of Ian's close friends. I'm putting you on speaker so we can discuss this as a group.'

The Headmaster placed the handset on his desk and pressed the speaker button. They could all hear the soft hiss of an open microphone.

'I have just received a letter in the mail,' said Mr Wainscott.

'How old-fashioned,' said Melanie.

'The message was spelled out in letters cut from a newspaper,' said Mr Wainscott. 'It read: I have kidnapped your son. I want five million dollars in unmarked bills. Get them ready to deliver by tomorrow night. Do not call the police.'

'My boy has been kidnapped!' wailed Mrs Wainscott, weeping mascara stains onto Uncle Bernie's clean shirt.

The Headmaster slumped back in his chair. 'Friday, you know Ian better than anyone else . . .'

'What about me? I'm his mother!' cried Mrs Wainscott.

'I don't mean to be offensive, Mrs Wainscott,' said the Headmaster, 'but children have a rat cunning and imagination for deceit that is inconceivable to ordinary adults, so Friday may have more insight into Ian's mind than any of us right now.'

'Plus, they're in love with each other,' said Melanie.

'What?!' exploded Mr Wainscott.

'She's just joking,' said the Headmaster, rubbing his forehead.

'No, I'm not,' said Melanie, looking confused.

Friday patted her reassuringly on the arm. 'We're focusing on the kidnapping now.'

'Is it possible that this whole thing has been masterminded by Ian himself?' asked the Headmaster.

'My boy has been kidnapped and you're blaming him?!' exclaimed Mr Wainscott.

'You have to understand, we have several faked kidnappings at this school every year,' said the Headmaster. 'Over-privileged children enjoy pretending to kidnap themselves. It gives them an excuse to bunk off school for a few days.'

'I don't think he faked it,' said Friday. 'You should have seen the look on his face when he opened the package. He always tries to play it cool, but he was so happy that his father was asking him to visit.'

'It must be someone who knew Ian well,' said Melanie. 'That's his one weakness. His need to be loved by his father.'

'Everyone wants to be loved by their father,' argued Friday.

'Yes, but most fathers are worth it,' said Melanie.

'Hey, I'm still on the line!' snapped Mr Wainscott through the speakerphone.

'I know,' said Melanie, 'I'd say the same thing if you were in the room.'

'Miss Priddock!' the Headmaster yelled out through his open office door. 'Get the police on the phone.'

'But the kidnapper said not to do that!' said Mrs Wainscott. 'Who knows what they'll do to Ian if you involve the police. They might cut off his finger and post it to me!' She collapsed on Uncle Bernie again, sobbing loudly.

'I'm sure they won't,' said Melanie. 'Everyone knows you don't have any money. It would be no good sending a finger to you, unless they were demanding vegetables from your garden.'

'If you are not prepared to pay the ransom,' said the Headmaster, 'then we will have to involve the police.'

Everyone was silent and stared at the phone. Mr Wainscott was silent too.

'Mr Wainscott,' said Friday, 'do you want to pay the ransom?'

'Five million dollars?!' exclaimed Mr Wainscott. 'I don't have that kind of money! Are you kidding me?!'

'Are you sure?' asked Melanie. 'You're always hiding money. Perhaps you stashed a diamond somewhere and forgot about it.'

'I don't have five million dollars,' said Mr Wainscott.

'But could you get hold of five million dollars?' asked Uncle Bernie. 'There are lots of ways an imaginative man such as yourself can come up with that sort of money.'

'No,' said Mr Wainscott. 'Besides, I thought you weren't supposed to give in to kidnappers. It only encourages them.'

'That's code for he doesn't *want* to put up five million dollars,' said Melanie, translating for Friday, who rarely understood conversational nuance.

'Then we'll have to bring in the police,' said the Headmaster.

Miss Priddock's weepy voice crackled over the intercom on the Headmaster's desk. 'Sergeant Crowley is on line two for you.'

'Are we agreed?' asked the Headmaster, looking across to Mrs Wainscott and Uncle Bernie. Mrs Wainscott still had her face buried in Uncle Bernie's shirt as she wept. Uncle Bernie nodded.

'What's happening?' Mr Wainscott's frustrated voice came over the speakerphone.

'People are nodding,' said Friday. 'But please don't expect me to narrate your phone call. I'm busy thinking hard.'

The Headmaster picked up the phone.

'Sergeant Crowley, I have a crime to report,' said the Headmaster.

Chapter 4

Things Get Serious

Things quickly escalated. Sergeant Crowley immediately realised this was the type of crime that was way out of his league. He struggled dealing with shoplifters and joy riders, so an international kidnapping and extortion demand was beyond him. He called in the Major Crime Squad.

The lead detective, Inspector Brenda Ray, interviewed Friday and Melanie exhaustively, which Friday rather enjoyed, and just made Melanie sleepy.

Inspector Ray was an impressive woman. She was elegant and efficient, and she had once been an elite level hurdler, so she had fearsomely strong quadriceps that could alone intimidate witnesses. Friday tried to explain to her that she was a detective savant. Inspector Ray was polite but disinterested.

'I'm sure I could be of help to your investigation,' argued Friday.

'How?' asked Inspector Ray.

'I could fly out to the Cayman Islands and look around,' said Friday. 'I'm fluent in French, so I could talk to the locals.'

'One child lost on an island full of tax exiles and smugglers is quite enough, thank you,' said Inspector Ray with a calmness she had clearly been trained to use with hysterical family members. 'My colleagues at the Cayman Islands police force will handle enquiries there. You can run along to class now.'

'But what are you going to be doing?' asked Friday.

Inspector Ray sighed. Her patience clearly wasn't as implacable as she might like it to be. 'I will be pursuing every angle of investigation,' she said, thinking that was as much explanation as Friday deserved.

'Will you forensically examine Mr Wainscott's business dealings to determine a list of his possible enemies?' asked Friday.

'Yes,' said Inspector Ray.

'Will you investigate Mrs Wainscott's former career as a lawyer?' asked Friday. 'Just in case this is actually an attempt to get revenge on her, perhaps for wrongly imprisoning someone for crimes they didn't commit?'

Inspector Ray ground her teeth together. 'We have limited resources,' she said.

'Ah,' said Melanie, 'that's code for she didn't think of that.'

'It is improper of me to discuss details of a case with two children,' snapped Inspector Ray.

'But we were the last people to see Ian,' said Friday, 'apart from the driver. Have you found him yet?'

'I only got handed this case two hours ago!' exclaimed Inspector Ray.

'But I gave you the licence plate of the vehicle,' said Friday.

'Police processes take time,' said Inspector Ray. 'They take even more time when members of the public are a nuisance.'

'She means you,' translated Melanie.

'That's not a very collaborative attitude,' said Friday.

'You are a child, I am a federal police inspector,' said Inspector Ray. 'We are not collaborating.'

'You probably should,' said Melanie. 'Friday is good at this sort of thing. And Ian is her kindred spirit, so they're psychically linked.'

Inspector Ray stood up and walked to the door. She called to a uniformed officer standing in the corridor. 'Drapalski, escort these two girls back to their class before I arrest them for interfering in a police investigation.'

Inspector Ray left to interview other, less irritating witnesses. Friday and Melanie ambled back to class with Constable Drapalski.

'I'm sure Ian's all right,' said Melanie.

'Really?' said Friday. 'I don't see why he would be. Kidnappers aren't usually known for being kind and considerate.'

'But if they want Mr Wainscott to pay, they're not going to harm him, are they?' said Melanie.

'But Mr Wainscott is never going to be able to pay,' said Friday. 'His money is never in the form of actual money. It's either "invested" in a dodgy scheme or hidden in some sort of transportable asset, like diamonds or postage stamps.'

'Perhaps the kidnapper is a lady and she'd quite like a diamond,' said Melanie.

'I just hope they're keeping him somewhere sanitary,' said Friday. 'They've done a good job of organising the kidnapping, I hope they've put as much planning into toilet facilities.'

'Don't worry, girls,' said Constable Drapalski. The girls had forgotten their escort was there. 'Inspector Ray is the best there is. If anyone is going to find your boyfriend, it will be her.'

Friday nodded.

'Aren't you going to say, "He's not my boyfriend"?' asked Melanie.

'What?' said Friday. She was caught up in her own thoughts.

'Never mind,' said Melanie. 'You've just had a relationship breakthrough, but we can talk about that later.'

Friday and Melanie heard nothing more throughout the day. There were plenty of police milling around the school, searching Ian's room and interviewing his friends. And there was a gaggle of media camped out on the front lawn. The Headmaster had tried to make them wait outside the front gate, but students kept sneaking down to sell them exclusive stories. So he thought it was better to have the journalists right outside the administration building, where he could keep an eye on them.

Students at Highcrest weren't allowed to have any sort of electronic devices, which generally didn't bother Friday. She wasn't one for keeping up with fashion or celebrity gossip, or even politics and world affairs, which to her mind were just about as frivolous compared to the greater issues of physics and the meaning of life. But on this one occasion, she really wanted to follow the news.

While other students were flirting with cameramen, Friday had a more practical approach to gaining information. She built herself a cathode-ray television set out of old equipment she found in the science storeroom, then tuned it to the local news station. This involved a lot of knob twiddling while they found the channel. And poor Melanie was inveigled into carrying a chain of wire coathangers around the room while Friday figured out the perfect configuration for their aerial. After ninety minutes of fiddling, the improvised television still had terrible vertical hold, but they could hear the sound well enough just in time for the intro music to the news bulletin.

'Shhh, it's starting,' said Friday.

'In leading news, floods in Preston have caused extensive damage to the local caravan park . . .' began the newsreader.

'It's a good job Ian can't hear this. He wouldn't be very gratified that he isn't the leading news story,' said Melanie.

'. . . And teenager Ian Wainscott remains missing. Police believe he was smuggled out of the country late yesterday. They are appealing for information from anyone who may have seen the boy. He is 182 centimetres tall, blonde-haired and of slim build.'

'Slim build?' said Friday.

'You're thinking of his rippling muscles again, aren't you?' said Melanie. 'Slim build is just code for not fat.'

The newsreader continued. 'In other news, Zhi Zhi the panda gave birth to triplets today –'

Friday switched the television off.

'Hey, I was listening to that!' protested Melanie. 'Pandas are my spirit animal. They nap almost as much as I do.'

'The police don't seem to be making much progress,' said Friday.

'What are you going to do?' asked Melanie. 'Will you try talking to Inspector Ray again?'

'There's no point,' said Friday. 'If Ian's already in the Cayman Islands, the answers are all there.'

'Then there's nothing you can do,' said Melanie.

'I can go to the Cayman Islands,' said Friday.

'The Headmaster said that's against school rules,' said Melanie.

'And I'm pretty sure I'm on an international watchlist,' added Friday. 'There's no way I'd get past airport security without an adult.'

'You could take Uncle Bernie,' said Melanie. 'He'd go with you.'

'He just got married today,' said Friday.

'It isn't going to be much of a honeymoon while his stepson is still kidnapped,' said Melanie.

'I hadn't thought of that,' said Friday. 'Ian is his son now.'

'*Stepson*,' qualified Melanie.

'That's a type of son,' said Friday, who was already heading over to her built-in wardrobe and pulling up the floorboards.

'The Headmaster knows that all the kids hide things under the floorboards,' said Melanie.

'So long as we hide things, he can't be accused of knowing about them,' said Friday as she pulled out her secret ham radio. Uncle Bernie had given it to her when she first went to Highcrest Academy. Technically it wasn't listed on the school's banned electronics register, but Friday hid it anyway to be on the safe side. She set it up on the desk, switched it on and started tuning it to the correct frequency.

'Grey Fedora, Grey Fedora, this is Green Pork Pie, do you read me? Over,' began Friday. 'Grey Fedora, Grey Fedora, come in. Over.'

'Would he be listening in?' asked Melanie.

'He always keeps his CB radio on,' said Friday. 'It's a habit from his police days. He likes monitoring what's going on. Grey Fedora, come in, please.'

The radio buzzed and beeped. 'There's a lot of static,' said Friday, adjusting the knobs to tune it better.

'Aamum . . . ot . . . ud . . . please,' came a voice through the static.

'What was that?' asked Melanie.

'I'm not sure,' said Friday. 'It could be a trucker, or someone out at sea. I don't know why they'd be on this frequency, though.'

'Barm . . . nit . . . hurr . . .' continued the static-addled voice. 'Shn . . . art . . . f . . .'

Friday adjusted the knobs subtly and suddenly the voice became clear: 'Help me! Friday, come in. Help me, please!'

'That's Ian's voice!' exclaimed Friday.

'But he's in the Cayman Islands,' said Melanie.

'Short-wave radio can travel massive distances,' said Friday.

'Hurry up,' said Melanie. 'Talk to him!'

Friday pressed the button on the mouthpiece. 'This is Friday. Ian, is that you?'

'Friday, thank goodness! You've got to help me,' said Ian. 'I've been kidnapped.'

'We know,' said Friday. 'The police have been here all day.'

'I'm being held on a boat,' said Ian. 'The guy who took me has fallen asleep. I broke out of my room and came up to the bridge, but I don't know where I am. There's no navigation system. And the kidnapper has the key. I can't operate the boat.'

'You could hot-wire it,' said Melanie.

'I don't know how to hot-wire a boat,' said Ian.

'I thought you could do all sorts of wicked things,' said Melanie.

'Hot-wiring a boat is not one of them,' said Ian. 'Besides, if I start the boat he's going to wake up. And this guy is crazy.'

'Has he hurt you?' asked Friday.

'No,' said Ian. 'He gave me a soda when I got in the car. There must have been sleeping pills in it. The next thing I knew, I woke up on this boat and it was dark.'

'The police assumed that the kidnapper was flying Ian to the Cayman Islands,' Melanie said to Friday, 'but instead they're sailing him there.'

'Don't worry, Ian,' said Friday. 'We'll find you. Is it cloudy where you are?'

'What difference does that make?' asked Ian.

'Can you see the stars?' asked Friday. 'If you can tell me what stars you see, I can work out where you are.'

'There's lots of stars, a whole sky full of them,' said Ian. 'How does that help if I don't know which way is north?'

'Just tell me what constellation is directly above you if you look straight up at the sky,' said Friday.

There was a pause.

'Orion,' said Ian, his voice crackling over the radio.

'Are you sure?' asked Friday.

'Yes, I'm directly below his belt,' said Ian.

'Are you certain you're not confusing it with another constellation?' asked Friday. 'Capricornia or Libra, perhaps?'

'I know Orion,' said Ian. 'It's the easiest one to spot. I'm directly below it.'

'Hold tight, we're on our way.' Friday checked her watch and turned to Melanie. 'It's 2.14 am. If Ian is directly below Orion's Belt, then I know exactly where he is. Let's go.'

'Where to?' asked Melanie. 'To call the police?'

'We'll radio them on the way,' yelled Friday over her shoulder as she ran out of the room.

Chapter 5

Rescue

Melanie was jogging along behind Friday. It was a testament to the depth of her friendship that she was moving at this increased speed. Melanie normally didn't jog. She didn't even care for walking quickly. But when Friday took off running towards the swamp, a flashlight in hand and her dressing gown flapping after her, Melanie just followed. She liked Friday, and Friday clearly needed help.

'Where are we going?' asked Melanie.

'The boatshed,' said Friday.

'Why?' asked Melanie.

'Because I'm not very good at swimming,' said Friday.

'I thought we were rescuing Ian,' said Melanie.

'We are,' said Friday.

'Then shouldn't we be calling the police?' said Melanie.

'We don't have a telephone,' said Friday. 'But there is a radio in Mr Pilcher's boat.'

The groundskeeper had an inflatable runabout boat. He mainly used it for fishing student property out of the swamp, or intercepting students who were trying to bunk off school by swimming out to their parents' luxury yachts anchored offshore.

Friday set to work picking the lock on the door of the boatshed. Melanie caught up to her and looked about. She grew up in a very wealthy family, so she was more used to boating than Friday. Melanie went around to the main jetty door and pulled on the handle. It was unlocked.

Friday came over when she heard the roller door go up. 'You're a genius,' she said to her friend.

'No, I just have insight into the way lazy boat owners think,' said Melanie.

'Do you know how to get the boat down into the water?' asked Friday.

'At home I would ask Jorge to do it,' said Melanie, 'but he isn't here. So I think we'll have to drag it in ourselves.'

'I'm sorry,' said Friday. She knew how much her friend didn't care for physical exertion.

'That's all right,' said Melanie. 'I like Ian too. Although obviously not *like*-like the way you do.'

On the whole, Friday thought they did a pretty good job of getting the boat out to sea (she only fell in the water twice). Melanie soon had it powered up and motoring out into open water.

'So where are we going?' asked Melanie.

'Just head straight out,' said Friday as she turned on the radio and tuned it to the police frequency.

'I'm pretty sure we have to go south to get to the Cayman Islands,' said Melanie, 'but don't ask me which direction that is. I know you can remember the points of the compass by saying, "Never Eat Soggy Wheat", but that's all I ever picked up in geography.'

'Ian isn't in the Cayman Islands,' said Friday. 'If my deductions are correct, he's just offshore from the school.'

'He is?!' exclaimed Melanie.

'He can see Orion directly above him,' said Friday. 'Look up!'

Melanie looked up. 'All I can see are stars.'

'Trust me, those stars above you are the constellation Orion,' said Friday.

'But surely a large chunk of the world can look straight up and see Orion at night?' said Melanie.

'Not right now,' said Friday. 'The earth and Orion are always moving. This is the only place on earth with this exact view. We know he's on a boat. So he has to be offshore somewhere here.'

'But how are you going to be able to spot him?' Melanie. 'It's pretty unlikely the kidnapper would be silly enough to leave on the lights on their boat if they're holding a hostage.'

'No, but Ian is awake and the kidnapper isn't. So perhaps Ian turned a light on,' said Friday. 'And he has – look!'

They could see a light flickering in the distance.

'Are you sure that's not just a phosphorescent fish?' asked Melanie.

'Good use of the word "phosphorescent" in a sentence,' said Friday.

'I thought so,' agreed Melanie. 'I've always liked the idea of animals that glow in the dark.'

'I'm pretty certain that's a boat light,' said Friday. 'It's clearly above the water, whereas a fish would be under the water.'

'Not if it was a flying phosphorescent fish,' said Melanie.

'There are no flying phosphorescent fish,' said Friday.

'Then we're really going to confront a kidnapper on the high seas, aren't we?' said Melanie.

'Hopefully we can avoid that if the kidnapper is a deep sleeper,' said Friday. 'Shhh, we're getting close. We don't want them to hear us.'

The girls stopped talking. They could just make out the shape of a boat up ahead in the moonlight.

'Won't the kidnapper hear our boat engine?' whispered Melanie.

'It's a constant sound,' said Friday. 'Maybe it will lull them in their sleep.'

'I don't find it very lulling, and usually anything could put me to sleep,' said Melanie.

'Well, we could turn the engine off,' said Friday. 'But then we'd have to row the rest of the way over to the boat.'

'Leave the engine on,' said Melanie. 'It's worth the risk.'

As they drew closer, the girls could make out that it was quite a fancy yacht.

'How are we going to get up on deck?' asked Friday. 'It must be four feet above water level. I didn't bring a grappling hook or a rope ladder.'

'Bring us around to the back of the yacht,' said Melanie. 'Yachts always have a ladder fixed around there. At least, they always have on all the yachts Daddy has owned.'

Friday steered the boat around to the rear of the yacht and, sure enough, there was a ladder attached to the back.

'Tie us on,' said Friday. She was still operating the engine, so Melanie picked up the rope at the nose of their boat and fastened it to the bottom rung.

'Let's go,' said Friday.

Melanie climbed up onto the yacht first. Friday left the engine idling and started making her way across the boat to the ladder. Unfortunately it was quite a choppy sea, so as Friday walked up the centre of the small boat, a large wave rolled through causing the boat to buck up. Because Friday was wearing her slippers (not recommended footwear for boating), she slipped and tumbled into the water with a big splash.

'Girl overboard!' cried Melanie. 'Friday, Friday! Where are you?'

Friday had been pulled away by the surge of the sea and was several metres from the boat. In the dark of night, Melanie couldn't see her anymore.

'Mel . . . blurgh!' spluttered Friday as she swallowed a mouthful of sea water while trying to call out to her friend.

Friday was not a strong swimmer at the best of times, but she particularly struggled when fully dressed in pyjamas plus a dressing gown in cold, churning water.

'Friday!' cried Melanie, a growing note of panic in her voice. 'Friday!'

Suddenly something flew straight over Melanie's head. She heard it fizz through the air above her. Melanie whipped around to see.

Silhouetted against the yacht's cabin light was Ian Wainscott, standing on the gunwale and athletically pulling in a rope hand over hand.

Melanie turned back to the sea. She could make out a bright orange buoyancy ring being dragged across the surface of the water, with her spluttering, bedraggled best friend clinging on to it for dear life. Ian lay down flat over the side of the yacht and grabbed Friday by the hand. Melanie clambered over to help. Together, they pulled Friday out of the water and onto the deck of the yacht. Friday collapsed there, gasping for breath for several moments.

'If this is a rescue attempt,' said Ian, 'it must be the worst rescue attempt ever.'

'We came for you, didn't we?' said Friday, before she had to stop speaking to cough up another lungful of seawater.

'I must admit, I've never been so happy to see two incompetent schoolgirls in their pyjamas motoring towards me in a boat,' said Ian with a smile.

'Let's get out of here before your kidnapper wakes up,' said Friday, getting to her feet.

They all went to the back of the yacht.

'Where's your boat?' asked Ian.

The dinghy was no longer tied to the ladder. There was no sign of it.

'It was right there,' said Friday. 'Melanie tied it up.'

Ian and Friday turned to Melanie.

'Melanie,' said Friday, 'you do know how to tie a knot, don't you?'

'Is there something to know?' asked Melanie. 'Whenever I've seen other people do it, it just looks like they're tangling it altogether.'

'This rescue attempt is getting better and better,' said Ian.

'I think he's being sarcastic,' Melanie informed Friday.

'Yes, I picked that up,' said Friday.

'So, basically,' said Ian, 'instead of just me being held hostage on this yacht in the middle of the sea, now all three of us are being held hostage on this yacht in the middle of the sea?'

'No,' said Friday, 'because the kidnapper doesn't realise we're here yet. Technically we're not hostages until they wake up.'

Just then, the door onto the deck burst open and a head popped through.

It was the driver who'd picked Ian up. As he climbed onto the deck, they could see that he wasn't smartly dressed now. The man was wearing pyjamas and carrying a frying pan in a menacing way that made it clear he wasn't intending to cook eggs.

'What's going on?' he demanded angrily.

'You've been kidnapped by a chauffeur?' marvelled Melanie.

'He's not really a driver,' said Ian. 'His name is Sam Fullerton. He knows my dad.'

'Who are these girls?' Fullerton demanded. 'How did they get here?'

Chapter 6

Newtonian Physics

'I am Friday Barnes, Girl Detective,' declared Friday, bravely standing to confront Fullerton.

'Ooh, I like the official title,' said Melanie.

'And I have come to rescue my friend Ian,' continued Friday.

'They're secretly in love,' explained Melanie.

'Not now, Melly,' said Ian.

'But they're in denial about it,' added Melanie.

'I can't hold you all hostage!' yelled Fullerton. 'Get out of here!'

'We can't, our boat escaped,' said Melanie.

'Lucky boat,' muttered Ian.

'I suppose you've got powerful parents too,' said Fullerton, looking Melanie and Friday over. 'They can make Wainscott pay me what he owes me.'

'Ah,' said Friday, turning to Ian. 'So your kidnapper is a disgruntled acquaintance of your father's?'

'Apparently Dad ruined him,' said Ian. 'Swindled him out of all his money. Leaving him with nothing but this yacht and the leased town car he kidnapped me in.'

'I'm not trying to steal anything!' yelled Fullerton. 'I just want back what's mine!'

'That's not quite true, is it?' said Friday. 'Because you've already stolen Ian.'

'How about you don't correct the semantics of the angry man with the frying pan?' suggested Ian.

'Sir,' said Friday, stepping forward, 'I can see that you have a valid case for your grievances.'

'You don't have to take his side,' said Ian.

'But your irrationally drastic course of action also leads me to believe,' Friday continued talking to Fullerton, 'that you are mentally unhinged.'

'Is that a scientific term?' asked Melanie.

'I thought it was politer to say than "bonkers",' said Friday.

'Can you please stop calling the kidnapper names?' pleaded Ian.

'I am taking control of this vessel,' declared Friday, 'and sailing back to Highcrest Academy, where you shall be handed over to the police.'

'Friday,' said Ian warningly, 'be careful. He's got a temper.'

'I don't care, these ridiculous shenanigans have gone on long enough,' said Friday as she decisively strode towards the bridge.

'No, you don't!' bellowed Fullerton as he lunged at her.

'Friday!' cried Melanie, covering her eyes so she wouldn't have to see something bad happen to her friend.

'No!' yelled Ian, lunging at Fullerton.

But in a move of surprising dexterity, Friday did not back away from Fullerton. Instead, she launched herself at him. Although, not the whole of him. She launched herself at his feet, dropping to a ball on the ground just as he hit maximum speed so that he tripped over her, slammed into the gunwale with so much momentum that he toppled straight over the side and landed with an enormous splash in the water.

'Did you plan that?' asked Ian, astonished.

'I saw something similar on a *Road Runner* cartoon,' said Friday. 'At the time I thought it was an improbable – but not impossible – use of Newtonian physics.'

'Help!' spluttered Fullerton. 'Help!'

'Why should we help you?' called Ian.

'Because leaving someone to die is technically manslaughter,' said Friday, throwing a buoyancy ring out to the man.

'But when he gets aboard he'll just try to overpower us again,' said Ian.

'Then we won't let him board,' said Friday, tying the end of the rope (much more effectively than Melanie had earlier) to the ladder at the rear of the boat. 'Melanie, do you know how to drive a yacht?'

'I do, actually,' said Melanie.

'Then take us full speed back to the school,' said Friday.

'Which way is that?' asked Melanie.

'You see that yellow light in the distance?' said Friday, pointing to a far-off circle of light. 'That's the clock face of the school tower. Aim for that. You'll see the light on the jetty when we get closer.'

'What about him?' asked Ian. Fullerton had swum most of the way to the boat.

'Sir, we are not going to allow you to reboard,' said Friday. 'So I suggest you grab hold of the buoyancy ring.'

'What?' said Fullerton.

'We're taking you back to the school,' said Friday, 'but we're not allowing you back on the boat, because you're deeply unpleasant and we don't trust you.'

'But it's my boat!' yelled Fullerton.

'We're not going to damage it,' said Friday, 'because soon you'll need to sell it to cover your legal fees.'

At this point, Melanie had obviously figured out all the controls because she gunned the engine and the expensive yacht took off at full speed.

'Hey!' yelled Fullerton.

'Grab the ring!' yelled Friday.

The man reached out and grabbed the orange ring as it whipped past him. The yacht was moving fast.

He had to hug the ring close to his chest to hold on as he was dragged along the surface of the water, skimming on his belly.

Ian was able to use the yacht's radio to contact the police. By the time Melanie slowed the boat for its final approach to the school jetty, there was quite a crowd waiting for them. Sergeant Crowley was there. He had driven his squad car all the way down the lawn to the jetty. The lights on his car were flashing, giving an unexpected party feel to the dark night.

'That's going to annoy Mr Pilcher,' observed Friday. 'He's going to have a tricky time getting the tyre tracks out of the grass.'

Soon they were alerted to the presence of Mrs Wainscott.

'Sausage!' she shrieked.

Ian groaned.

Melanie giggled.

'My baby, my poor baby!' cried Mrs Wainscott.

'He looks fine,' said Uncle Bernie, trying to calm his new wife.

'He's probably in shock, permanently trauma-tised,' predicted Mrs Wainscott hysterically.

'What's she even doing here?' asked Ian.

'Friday didn't tell you?' asked Melanie.

'Tell me what?' asked Ian.

Friday stomped on Melanie's foot.

'Ow,' said Melanie. 'You just stood on my foot. Oh, I see. You stood on my foot as a subtle signal to get me to stop talking.'

'Tell me what?' repeated Ian.

'It's not for me to say,' said Friday. 'You need to talk to your mother.'

'About what?' asked Ian. 'Oh no.' He was staring at Uncle Bernie now. 'Why is your uncle wearing a suit?'

As soon as Ian stepped onto the jetty, Mrs Wainscott fell on him, weeping. 'My baby, my poor, poor baby.'

'I bet you wish she was calling you "Sausage" now,' said Melanie.

'Where's the perpetrator?' asked Sergeant Crowley.

'His name is Sam Fullerton,' said Friday. 'He's behind the boat, in the buoyancy ring.'

Sergeant Crowley went around to the back of the yacht and panned a flashlight across the water.

'What buoyancy ring?' he asked.

'He can't have gone anywhere,' said Friday. 'He was right there a moment ago as we approached the school.' She hurried to the back of the boat and leaned over. She grabbed the rope and started pulling it in. But the rope came too quickly. Soon she was holding the empty end of the rope in her hand.

'You lost him?' said Sergeant Crowley.

'In my defence, our priority was rescuing Ian, not detaining a violent criminal,' said Friday.

'Although Friday did a really clever self-defence move she learned from the Road Runner,' said Melanie.

'He can't have gone far,' said Uncle Bernie.

'Are you kidding?' asked Mrs Wainscott. 'Sam Fullerton is a former Olympic swimmer. He came seventh in the breaststroke at the Seoul games. He could be miles away by now.'

'You know the man who kidnapped me?' asked Ian.

'Of course, so do you,' said Mrs Wainscott. 'He was your father's groomsman at our wedding. He's your godfather.'

'And Dad ripped him off?' said Ian.

'Your dad rips everyone off, darling,' said Mrs Wainscott. 'You know he doesn't mean it personally.'

'You three get up to the school and get warm. I'll come and take your statements as soon as I can,' said Sergeant Crowley. 'I'm going to get the water police and the recruits from the academy to come down here and make a full search of the swamp and the bay. I'd better call Inspector Ray. She's not going to like this. But we'll find him, don't you worry.'

Friday, Melanie and Ian started walking back to the school with Mrs Wainscott, Uncle Bernie and the Headmaster. Friday hadn't realised she was cold until now. The adrenalin must have given her the illusion of warmth, but now that things were starting to return to normality she realised she was freezing. Pretty soon, even her teeth began to chatter. Then suddenly she was enveloped in total warmth that smelled like pizza, coffee and breath mints. Uncle Bernie had draped his jacket around her shoulders.

'Have you been eating pizza in your best suit?' asked Friday.

Uncle Bernie smiled. 'Maybe a little.'

'You make me sick,' said Ian.

'I didn't know you disliked pizza,' said Melanie.

'You're taking advantage of my mother when she's fragile and vulnerable!' accused Ian.

'What?' said Uncle Bernie.

'You've married her, haven't you!' demanded Ian. 'Don't try to deny it. I can see the rings you're both wearing.'

Uncle Bernie didn't say anything. But even in the darkness of the moonlit night, they could see he was blushing red.

'Are Mum and Dad even divorced properly yet?' asked Ian. 'I thought there was paperwork to process.'

'Oh, sweetheart,' said Mrs Wainscott, 'that all happened months ago. I didn't like to say anything in case it upset you.'

'Months ago?' said Ian. 'But Dad hasn't been in jail that long.'

'Yes, that's the other thing we didn't tell you,' said Mrs Wainscott. 'Your father and I started the divorce paperwork a year and a half ago, long before he got arrested.'

'Why wasn't I told?' asked Ian.

'Well, you were here at school,' said Mrs Wainscott. 'We didn't want to distract you from your studies.'

The Headmaster made a snorting noise.

Uncle Bernie glared at him.

'Sorry,' said the Headmaster. 'Ian is undoubtably very bright and capable, but he isn't that diligent a student.'

'We've come to pick you up,' said Mrs Wainscott to her son. 'We thought you'd like to come with us on our honeymoon trip.'

'How nauseating,' said Ian.

'Hey, don't be rude to your mum,' said Uncle Bernie.

'You're not the boss of me,' said Ian.

'No, but I love your mum and I don't want you to upset her,' said Uncle Bernie.

'She's my mum!' yelled Ian. 'I get to upset her whenever and wherever I like!' He turned and stomped off in another direction.

'Poor Ian,' said Melanie. 'Do you think he realises he's walking off towards the rugby pitches?'

'I'm sure he'll figure it out and double back when he thinks we're not looking,' said Friday.

Chapter 7

▬▬▬▬▬▬▬▬▬▬▬▬▬▬

Permission to Skive

It was a forlorn couple of weeks at Highcrest Academy. At least, for Ian it was. He had refused to go with his mum and Uncle Bernie (his stepdad, as Ian refused to think of him) on their honeymoon. Uncle Bernie asked Friday if she still wanted to come, but Friday suggested that they could all celebrate later, when Ian had had a chance to get used to the idea. It would just rub salt in the wound if she was on holiday with his mother, while he was upset.

'It's strange to see Ian so sad,' said Melanie as they sat in the dining hall, eating lunch. Friday looked up to see Ian on the far side of the room, half-heartedly picking at his peach cobbler.

'What do you mean?' asked Friday. 'He gets upset all the time. He's a classic sulky, stroppy teenager.'

'Classically handsome, perhaps,' said Melanie. 'But normally when he gets upset he gets angry, nasty and vindictive. This time he's just quiet. I think I prefer him when he's spiteful. After all, that's the Ian you fell in love with.'

'I did not,' said Friday.

'No, you were able to see through it, to the pain of the abandoned boy beneath,' agreed Melanie. 'But now that's all there is left. I miss his anger – he had such creative ways of expressing his annoyance with people.'

'Like the time he put my clothes on top of a channel marker, or the time he attached an electric motor to the picnic table I was sitting on and drove it into the swamp, or the time he imploded my pencil box?' asked Friday.

'Yes,' agreed Melanie, smiling fondly. 'Good times.'

Friday rolled her eyes. There was no point trying to reason with Melanie.

'I just hope he snaps out of it before we go to camp next week,' said Melanie.

Friday groaned. 'I can't believe I didn't read the prospectus carefully enough,' she said. 'If I'd known about this camp in advance, I would have seriously considered homeschooling myself.'

'Camp isn't so bad,' said Melanie. 'All that fresh air is good for you.'

'Really? You're advocating outdoor activity?' asked Friday.

'Of course,' said Melanie. 'Fresh air helps you sleep at night.'

'You always sleep like a log,' said Friday.

'Yes, but it's a better quality of sleep when teachers haven't been trying to fill my head with maths and science and history all day,' said Melanie. 'It's the pure restful type of sleep you only get when all you've been doing is watch other people chop wood.'

'I really want to sprain my ankle so I don't have to go,' said Friday.

'So why don't you?' asked Melanie. 'Obviously you shouldn't actually sprain your ankle, but you could always pretend to do it.'

'Because I'm frightened,' confessed Friday.

'Of woodchopping?' asked Melanie. 'I don't blame you. I don't know how it is that so few students accidentally chop their toes off. Speaking of which, did you know that Pandora Benedetti had to have a toe surgically reattached after the last camp?'

'No, I'm not scared of that,' said Friday. 'An axe swinging through the air is just the mathematics of parabolic motion. I'm not scared of parabolic motion. Besides, I haven't got the strength to lift an axe, so there's no way I could hurt myself with one. I'm scared of the situation. Ten people in a dorm – not just you and me – working in teams and overcoming obstacles as a group. I'm terrible at all that human interaction stuff.'

'Then why don't you skive off?' asked Melanie.

'Because I learn so little at school,' said Friday. 'There's almost nothing the teachers tell us that I don't know already. I completely grasp the mathematical and scientific principles up to university level and beyond. The greatest lesson I learn from school is how to interact with other people.'

'Really?' said Melanie. 'Because if that's the case, you're not doing too well at your studies.'

'I know,' said Friday, 'which is why I shouldn't shirk this challenge. I should go to camp precisely because I really don't want to go. I need to face my fear of social interaction.'

'Good for you,' said Melanie. 'And on the bright side, if you don't overcome your fear of social inter-action, you will learn how to use an axe. Once you can swing an axe about, you don't need to socially interact with anyone you don't want to.'

'Barnes!' called the Headmaster. He was waddling towards them at an accelerated speed.

'Why must everyone use my surname?' asked Friday.

'Because your first name is so silly,' said Melanie.

Friday nodded. Even she had to acknowledge this was true. The Headmaster reached them.

'I want to talk with you,' said the Headmaster.

'Because you want her to come up with a gambling system that actually works and allows you to systemat-ically beat the odds at the racetrack?' guessed Melanie.

'No,' said the Headmaster. 'Risk is the best bit about gambling. If I got a brilliant mathematician to work out a system that worked, it would totally ruin the fun of it.'

'Then why do you need to speak to me?' asked Friday. 'Do you need help with a problem?'

'In a way, yes,' said the Headmaster.

'What's the problem?' asked Friday.

'You,' said the Headmaster.

'I haven't done anything,' said Friday.

'Not yet, no,' said the Headmaster. 'But we all know it's only a matter of time before you uncover something, or expose something, or entrap somebody, or just say something unnecessarily rude.'

'Usually when I do those things it's because I'm solving a case for you,' said Friday.

'Yes, I know, but now I want you to stop it,' said the Headmaster. 'I'm asking you to consider not going to camp.'

'Why?' asked Friday.

'Because it took me years to find this new camp,' said the Headmaster. 'Most of the other camps refuse to take Highcrest Academy because the children are so obnoxious, their pranks are so dangerous, and at least three students always get lost in the woods.'

'Then why does the school persevere with the program?' asked Friday.

'Because the parents love it,' said the Headmaster. 'They delight in it when their kids come home sunburnt, their hands covered in blisters and legs covered in leech bites. They think it's "character-building". Sometimes I think parents are even bigger sadists than maths teachers.'

'Do the maths teachers know that's how you think of them?' asked Friday.

'Of course,' said the Headmaster. 'If they didn't enjoy being reviled, they wouldn't have become maths teachers. Anyway, that's beside the point. I can't have you offending the staff and getting our whole school banned. We're lucky, because Camp Courage was going to bar us too. But someone persuaded the woman who runs the place to give us a chance.'

'This is so unfair,' said Friday. 'I'm not a student who plays pranks or gets up to mischief. I'm always the one solving those problems.'

'I know,' said the Headmaster, 'and I am very grateful. But you have such a charmless, tact-free way of solving problems, the solution often ends up being much worse. So I think it would be better for everyone if you spent the four weeks here. You could help Mrs Cannon. She's going to use the time to rearrange the book depository.'

'You know that means she's just going to take naps in the English room closet, don't you?' said Friday.

'Of course I know that!' snapped the Headmaster. 'This is exactly my point. Mrs Cannon says she is organising. I pretend I think that's true. We're both happy. You pointing out the truth doesn't help anyone.'

'You are a very deceptive man, Headmaster,' said Friday.

'All polite people are,' said the Headmaster. 'It's called "being nice". You should try it sometime.'

'Friday doesn't mean to upset people,' said Melanie kindly.

'I know that, you know that, but the wilderness survival experts who run Camp Courage don't know that,' said the Headmaster. 'I can't have you upsetting them.'

'I refuse to refuse to go,' said Friday. 'I am exercising my right as a full-fee paying student to attend camp.'

'You haven't actually paid any fees since first semester,' said the Headmaster.

'I've paid for them with services rendered,' said Friday. 'There are several criminals behind bars that are testament to that fact.'

'Very well, go to camp if you must,' said the Headmaster. 'But please, I'm begging you, try not to talk to any of the counsellors.'

'Couldn't she talk to them nicely?' asked Melanie.

'I think that is beyond her,' said the Headmaster. 'It would be better if Friday didn't speak. And please don't go around uncovering any crimes.'

'You want me to let crime go unchallenged?' asked Friday.

'Yes,' said the Headmaster. 'Yes, please.'

'What if there is a serious crime?' asked Friday.

'Try closing your eyes and counting to ten to see if it just goes away,' said the Headmaster.

'As a scientist, I refuse to turn a blind eye to hard facts,' said Friday.

'If you manage to get all the way through the four weeks of camp without calling the police in,' said the Headmaster, 'I will give you a whole free term of tuition next year.'

'I'm already paid up halfway through next year,' said Friday.

'What do you want, then?' asked the Headmaster.

Friday thought about it for a moment. 'Salted caramel ice-cream for dinner once a week,' she decided.

'Deal,' said the Headmaster. And they shook hands on it.

━━━━━━━━━━━━━━━━━━━━━

Chapter 8

The Wheels on the Bus Don't Always Go Round and Round

The bus ride to camp was quite something. Many of the privileged students had never been on a bus before. Some were excited by the novelty while others, like Mirabella Peterson, were disgusted by the hygiene implications.

Mirabella stood blocking the entry of the bus, refusing to get on. She was a very pretty and surprisingly athletic girl who had a talent for getting her own way, largely through being sulky and petulant.

She wore false eyelashes, even during PE, and although it was against school rules, none of the teachers said anything about it because no one could be bothered dealing with one of her tantrums.

'How do I know if the seat is clean?' demanded Mirabella Peterson.

'My dear,' said the Headmaster, trying to draw on his last ounce of patience, 'I can assure you that millions, if not billions, of people around the world travel on buses every day without coming to any harm.'

'That's my point,' said Mirabella. 'Millions of people with all their germs have been touching the seats.'

Friday was close behind in the gaggle of students waiting to get on. She found Mirabella an intriguing psychological case study.

'Rosa Parks fought for the right for African Americans to sit where they liked on buses, because it represented the small entrenched acts of racism that oppressed people of colour,' said Friday. 'But you're fighting for the right not to sit on a bus seat in case you catch a cold, because it represents how selfish you are.'

'Yes,' said Mirabella, 'that's exactly right.'

'I've got hand sanitiser,' said Trea Babcock. 'Would you like some?'

'Yes, please,' said Mirabella. 'I'm going to tell my parents about this. The school should be providing hand sanitiser.'

Trea Babcock rifled through her bag and found her hand sanitiser. It was a two-litre pump-action bottle.

'Where on earth did you get a bottle of hand sanitiser that big?' asked the Headmaster.

'They don't even have bottles that big in hospitals,' said Friday.

'Which is probably why they have so many golden staph outbreaks,' said Melanie.

'Mummy sent it to me,' said Trea. 'She didn't want me to catch germs from any wildlife.'

'You do realise that very few germs can be spread between species?' said Friday.

'I don't think she was worried about me catching germs from another species,' said Trea. 'I think her idea of wildlife is teenage boys.'

'Fair enough,' said Friday. She could see how dipping Trea Babcock in antiseptic gel would curtail the spread of disease.

After liberally dabbing hand sanitiser on her seat, and on the surrounding handrail and window, Mirabella finally sat down, which meant the rest of the seventh graders could shuffle onto the bus.

Friday and Melanie sat towards the front.

Ian was still being grouchy so he skulked straight past them and sat right up the back.

'So this is how poor people travel,' said Melanie, looking about.

'Some poor people,' said Friday. 'Really poor people walk.'

'How horrendous,' said Melanie. 'Thank goodness Mummy and Daddy are rich. Where is the hostess?'

'The what?' asked Friday.

'The hostess,' said Melanie. 'Or is it "steward"? You know, the person who serves the in-journey meal.'

'This is a bus,' said Friday. 'There is no in-journey meal.'

'Gosh,' said Melanie. She looked up and down the aisle. 'Friday, where is the bathroom?'

Friday reached out and held her friend's hand. 'There isn't one.'

Melanie gasped.

'Don't worry,' said Friday. 'You'll be okay. You can make it. Besides, if you really need to go, I'm sure the bus driver will be able to pull over so you can pee behind a bush.'

'Friday, I'm frightened,' said Melanie.

'You're going to be fine,' said Friday reassuringly. 'Why don't you go to sleep? You're always happier when you're asleep.'

'Good idea,' said Melanie, closing her eyes. She was obviously very nervous because it took her three minutes to drift into slumber, which was two minutes longer than it normally did.

Camp Courage was a four-hour drive from Highcrest Academy. The road there was smooth and the countryside was monotonous, so soon even Friday was starting to drift off.

Friday was in a half-asleep state, dreaming that she was in a university laboratory discovering the 119th unique element when suddenly she heard screaming. It took her giant brain a few seconds to realise that the screaming was not one of joy at her scientific breakthrough – it was someone screaming in terror.

Friday leapt up and turned around. Mirabella Peterson was sitting many rows behind her, wailing as loud as she could. From this distance, Friday could see that Mirabella still had two arms and a head, and there was no blood spraying out from anywhere, so it was not immediately apparent why the girl was making such a bloodcurdling noise.

'What's going on?' demanded Friday as she strode down the bus, assuming the position of authority figure because the only adult there was Mr Maclean, the geography teacher, who everyone agreed could not cope with normal day-to-day life let alone a crisis.

Mirabella didn't answer. She just kept screaming.

'It's her hair,' said Melanie. She had woken up and followed Friday down the bus.

Friday looked closely at Mirabella's hair. Friday was not a hair person. She could not be less interested in the subject. She was barely motivated to comb her own hair, let alone notice the style of others. But now, as she examined it, she observed that Mirabella had a large bald patch on the top of her head.

'Did she have that before?' Friday whispered to Melanie.

Melanie shook her head.

'Is that a fashionable style?' asked Friday.

Melanie's eyes widened and she shook her head again. 'Not since the medieval monk look went out of style.'

'What happened?' Friday asked Mirabella.

But Mirabella just kept wailing. Friday looked around at the people sitting near her. 'What happened?' Friday repeated.

Everyone looked at her blankly.

'Someone attacked me!' screamed Mirabella.

'Who?' asked Friday.

'I don't know,' said Mirabella. 'I was asleep.'

'Was it a good sleep?' asked Melanie. 'I was asleep too and having a lovely dream about hot chips.'

'When I woke up someone had chopped my hair off,' said Mirabella.

'Only a portion of it,' said Friday.

'A portion on the top that everyone can see!' said Mirabella.

'What's all this, then?' asked Mr Maclean. He had walked down the bus, having decided that he could no longer ignore the commotion. He had to pretend to be a responsible adult at some point.

'Someone has given Mirabella an unattractive haircut while she was sleeping,' said Friday. 'But no one will admit who.'

'Trea, you must have seen something,' said Mr Maclean. Trea was sitting directly behind Mirabella. 'What happened?'

'I don't know,' said Trea. 'I was turned around, playing cards with Klara.' She pointed to the girl behind her who nodded.

'What about you?' Mr Maclean asked Bethany, who was sitting next to Trea.

'I don't know,' said Bethany. 'I had my eyes closed. I was meditating. My psychologist tells me I need to breathe less.'

'I can vouch for that,' said Trea. 'Her deep breathing was totally annoying.'

'Then it must have been someone from the front,' said Mr Maclean. He turned around and glared at the students in the front half of the bus. 'Come on, admit it. Who did it?'

'It couldn't have been anyone from there,' said Friday. 'The aisle is too narrow. I would have felt them brush past.'

'What if it was an incredibly skinny person?' asked Melanie.

'I still would have sensed the movement of them passing by,' said Friday. 'It must have been someone from the rear.'

Rajiv Patel snorted.

'What are you giggling about, Patel?' demanded Mr Maclean.

'Friday said "rear". You know, as in "bottom",' explained Patel.

Now half the bus chortled.

'That's it,' said Mr Maclean. 'Patel, I want you to write two hundred lines – "I will not make rude jokes".'

'But we're going to camp,' said Patel. 'We don't have pens and paper.'

'You can scratch it in the dirt when you get there,' said Mr Maclean.

Friday turned to the girl sitting directly in front of Mirabella. 'What about you, Moiya? If someone was giving Mirabella an impromptu haircut right behind you, you must have noticed something.'

'I was reading a book,' said Moiya.

'You were?' said Friday, genuinely surprised. She didn't often come across a Highcrest Academy student voluntarily reading a book.

'Yes, she was reading it aloud to me,' said Twiggy, the girl sitting across the aisle from Moiya.

'It must be a very good one to have you both so totally absorbed,' said Friday.

'It is,' said Moiya, showing her the cover. 'It's a book of horoscopes. It tells me exactly what will happen in my life, day by day, for an entire year.'

Friday stared at Moiya before turning to Melanie. 'Is she joking?'

Melanie shook her head.

'You do realise that planetary movements may affect tide and gravity, but in no way do they affect personality let alone life events?' said Friday.

'Yes, they do!' said Moiya. 'Look at my horoscope for today: Your faith will be challenged by another. But you will be strong and ignore them. Avoid the colour brown.'

Friday glanced down at her signature brown cardigan. 'That doesn't mean anything.'

'It's good advice, though,' said Trea with a snigger.

'So none of you saw anything?' asked Friday. She glanced about at all the blank faces surrounding her. No one looked particularly innocent, but nobody looked particularly guilty, either. There was no red-faced shame, or telltale attempts to avoid eye contact.

'Mirabella, do you have any enemies?' asked Friday.

'Of course not,' said Mirabella. 'I'm one of the most popular girls in school.'

Melanie snorted. Friday looked at her.

'Sorry,' said Melanie. 'The funny part is she's not lying. She actually believes that's true.'

'So you haven't annoyed or insulted anybody, or made someone jealous recently?' asked Friday, turning back to Mirabella.

'I hope I have,' said Mirabella. 'That's what being popular is all about. Making people die with jealousy.'

Friday was confused. She turned back to Melanie. 'She doesn't understand the definition of the word "popular", does she?'

'Oh, she does,' said Melanie. 'It's just that her definition is not one you'd find in any dictionary.'

'Half the girls in the lacrosse team wanted to scratch my eyes out when I got picked as captain again,' began Mirabella, 'Barbara Trieste cried for a week after I snogged her boyfriend on a dare in the first week of term, and Wai-Yi Yap was annoyed when I copied her history answers, then got a higher mark because the teacher liked me more. And Jessica Dawes has never forgiven me for wearing the same dress as her to her pool party last summer. And then . . .'

'I get the picture,' said Friday. 'It's going to be a long list of suspects. I'll have to get to the bottom of this another way, with a forensic examination of the crime scene.'

'It's a crowded bus travelling at a hundred kilometres an hour,' said Bethany. 'You can't ask us to step outside.'

'The driver could stop the bus,' said Friday.

'He will not,' said Mr Maclean. 'I don't care if every student on this bus is shaved bald – we will not delay this trip. I've got to see to it that you're dropped off so I can get back to school.'

'Why, do you have a date tonight, sir?' giggled Trea.

'No, I want to savour every moment of not having you grotty year 7 students clogging up our school,' said Mr Maclean.

'Did he just call us grotty?' asked Bethany.

Mirabella started crying again.

'Don't get angry with Mr Maclean,' said Melanie soothingly. 'It was a poor choice of words, but he is a geography teacher so his vocabulary probably isn't very large.'

'If you pick your feet up, I'll investigate,' said Friday, dropping to her knees and crawling under

Bethany's legs so she could check the floor around Mirabella.

'What can you see?' asked Melanie.

'Not much,' said Friday. 'It's pretty dark down here. I wish I had my headlamp, but it's stowed in my suitcase under the bus.'

'We're not stopping to get it out,' growled Mr Maclean.

'Okay,' said Friday. She didn't want to stay on the floor any longer than she had to. The floor of a school bus is a wildly unhygienic place. And Bethany seemed to be swinging her feet into Friday's back more than she needed too. 'There's hair everywhere down here.'

Mirabella wailed.

'It's under this seat, the one in front and the one behind,' said Friday.

'The bus is moving about,' said Mr Maclean. 'The hair would have rolled back and forth while Mirabella was sleeping.'

'Hmm,' said Friday. 'And where is the weapon?'

'You mean the scissors?' said Mr Maclean. 'There's no need to be melodramatic.'

'Cutting someone's hair without their permission is assault,' said Friday. 'Therefore the implement used may be considered a weapon. Especially if it really was a weapon, like a knife.'

'You're not suggesting one of these students has a knife, are you?' spluttered Mr Maclean. 'They're against school rules.'

'Someone here has some sort of cutting implement and the lack of scruples to use it,' said Friday, 'and they wouldn't want to be discovered with the device, so where could they have hidden it?'

'It could be anywhere,' said Melanie. 'In a seat pocket, embedded in a cushion, or tucked behind the wall lining.'

'But it would eventually be discovered,' said Friday. 'If it were me, I'd throw it out the window.'

Friday leaned over and pulled the window open. Only the small part at the top slid open. But it was plenty of room to throw an object out.

'Then you'll never find it,' said Mr Maclean.

Suddenly the bus jolted and Mr Maclean was thrown sideways, knocking Friday into Mirabella and Bethany's laps.

'Get off!' yelled Bethany.

'You're crushing me!' accused Mirabella.

Melanie just sat down on the floor in the aisle.

The bus continued to swerve, first one way then the other, as the driver desperately tried to regain control of the vehicle. He was grinding through the gears and stomping on the compression brakes as he eventually brought the bus to a shuddering halt.

It took some time for Friday to disentangle herself and make it down the aisle of the bus, over and around discombobulated students. By the time she got outside, the bus driver was already inspecting the damage. He was standing behind the bus, hands on hips, shaking his head. Friday jogged over to join him. She could immediately see the problem. One of the tyres was as flat as a pancake. It was no wonder the driver struggled to control the vehicle.

'They're brand new tyres,' said the driver. 'They only went on last week. Top-quality steel-belted radials. I don't know how this could've happened.'

'You must have driven over something,' said Friday.

'Out here on the freeway?' said the driver. 'There's nothing on the road. And if there is, you can always see it from so far away you can change lanes to avoid it.'

'Something must have punctured the tyre,' said Friday, crouching down to inspect the rubber.

She couldn't see anything, so she ran her hand over the tread to check if she could feel anything.

'I told you there's nothing there,' said the driver.

'Could you roll the bus forward a metre?' asked Friday. 'Perhaps there's something on the underside of the tyre.'

The bus driver grumpily went back to his driver's seat, started the engine and rolled the bus forward just a little.

'There's something here!' cried Friday. She looked closely at a piece of metal embedded in the tread. It was thin and about two centimetres long.

'What is that?' asked Mr Maclean. He and Melanie had come to find out what was happening.

'Hmm,' said Friday. 'I have my suspicions. But let's find out for sure.' She removed a large penknife-style tool from her pocket.

'You can't carry that!' exclaimed Mr Maclean. 'It's a dangerous weapon.'

'We're going to a wilderness camp,' said Friday. 'A utility tool is going to be handy.'

'Give it to me,' said Mr Maclean.

'No,' said Friday. 'If I wanted to hurt another student, I could just hit them with a rock.'

'It would be better to take your sock off, put the rock in the bottom and then use that to hit them,' said Melanie.

Everyone turned to look at her.

'What?' said Melanie.

'Nice use of applied physics,' said Friday.

'I learned that from watching prison dramas,' said Melanie. 'If you're going to the pokey, you need to know how to bust heads.'

'True. It's a valuable life skill,' agreed Friday as she opened the utility tool to the pliers function. 'You see, Mr Maclean, it's just a harmless pair of pliers for removing a nail or, in this case . . .' Friday grabbed the object with the pliers and pulled hard, only to stumble backwards and land on her bottom as she yanked out . . .

A small pair of scissors.

'What is that?' asked Mr Maclean.

'It looks like nail scissors,' said Friday, peering at them closely. 'I don't believe it!'

'What?' asked Melanie.

'There's a name etched on the handle,' said Friday. 'It says . . . Mirabella Peterson.'

'Right, that's it,' said Mr Maclean. He looked up and spotted Mirabella through the window.

He banged on the toughened glass. 'Mirabella, get down here right now!'

Mirabella sulkily made her way out of the bus and over to where they were standing. The driver had started to get out the jack and spare tyre.

'What is the meaning of this?' demanded Mr Maclean, waving the scissors in Mirabella's face.

'Careful, sir,' said Melanie, 'you shouldn't wave scissors. You could poke Mirabella's eye out.'

Mr Maclean glared at Melanie. He looked as if he would quite like to poke her eye out. He turned back to Mirabella.

'Why were these scissors embedded in this tyre?' asked Mr Maclean.

'I don't know,' said Mirabella. 'Why should I?'

'They're your scissors!' yelled Mr Maclean. 'Your name's on them.'

'Really?' said Mirabella, taking a better look. 'That would be Consuela. She's the new maid. She's grateful not to be living in a fishing village in the Philippines anymore. She's got a very good work ethic. She doesn't want to be sent home before her visa gets renewed.'

'Why did you jam them in the tyre?' asked Mr Maclean.

'I didn't!' said Mirabella. 'I've never touched a tyre in my life.'

'Not even a bicycle tyre?' asked Melanie.

'Goodness, no,' said Mirabella. 'We never ride bikes. Only ponies.'

'Sir, look, there's some hair trapped between the blades,' said Friday as she closely inspected the scissors.

'Don't be disgusting, Barnes,' said Mr Maclean contemptuously.

'But it is clearly Mirabella's hair,' said Friday. 'No one else has that uniquely artificial shade of blonde.'

Mirabella smiled and nodded proudly. 'My stylist blends the peroxide herself.'

'Yes, that is a ridiculous statement for so many reasons,' said Friday. 'Most of them to do with chemistry, so I won't bother explaining them to you. But my point is, these were the scissors used to cut Mirabella's hair. Then, once the crime was committed, in a thoughtless attempt to hide the evidence, the perpetrator must have thrown the scissors out of the window of the bus. The bus was travelling at one hundred kilometres per hour. That creates a significant draught, drawing air at high speed around the shell of the vehicle, which in turn would have sucked the scissors back in towards the bus, so they embedded in the tyre and then were pressed further in by the rotation of the wheel.'

'Who would do such a thing?' said Mr Maclean. 'It's days like this that make me really hate children. All I had to do was chaperone you out to the camp, then I could go back to the school and enjoy an afternoon off. But no. I have to put up with this.' Mr Maclean threw his hands in the air in frustration. 'Tell me who did it and I'll see if I can get them expelled or, at the very least, suspended.'

Friday looked up at the bus. Forty faces were looking down at her. Some were smiling and giggling, and while she couldn't hear them, they were clearly passing nasty comments amongst themselves.

'Apparently no one,' said Friday.

'What?!' exclaimed Mr Maclean. 'You're supposed to be the great detective. I thought you could work out anything.'

'I said *apparently* no one,' said Friday, 'because all the people who had the opportunity, those sitting immediately around Mirabella, they all back each other up. Trea and Klara provide each other with the alibi of playing cards, and they support Bethany's claim of meditating. Moiya and Twiggy cover for each other as well, because they both claim to have been engrossed in the horoscope book. And there is no way anyone else could have attacked Mirabella without one of those five girls noticing.'

'So who did it?' asked Mr Maclean.

'There's only one possible answer,' said Friday. 'They all did.'

'What?!' exclaimed Mr Maclean.

'They all did it,' said Friday. 'All five of them. It had to be one of them. And if they all say it was none of them, then they're all in on this together.'

'That's ridiculous,' said Mr Maclean.

'It is,' agreed Friday, 'but it's the only explanation that works. So no matter how silly it is, it must be true.'

'But they're my friends!' wailed Mirabella.

'Yes, but they're dreadful people,' said Melanie.

Mirabella nodded as she sobbed. Melanie was quite right.

'Trea, Klara and Twiggy, from the persistent bruises on their shins, I take it they're in the lacrosse team,' said Friday, 'that you captain?'

Mirabella nodded. 'They don't like it when I make them carry the equipment, so I do it all the time.'

'Bethany is Mirabella's roommate,' continued Friday, 'so no doubt she has a litany of grievances against her. And Moiya is Barbara Trieste's cousin, so she wouldn't appreciate Mirabella's reckless snogging.'

'It's amazing they didn't shave your eyebrows off as well,' said Melanie to Mirabella.

'So all five of them had the opportunity and the motive to commit the crime,' said Friday.

'You can't prove it,' said Mr Maclean glumly. 'There's no evidence.'

'Oh yes, there is,' said Friday. 'The hair was under all their seats.'

'But the movement of the bus would have made the hair slide around,' said Mr Maclean.

Friday sighed. 'Don't you have to study some basic physics to be a geography teacher?'

'What?' said Mr Maclean.

'Never mind,' said Friday. 'The answer is clearly no.'

'Friday,' said Melanie, 'maybe you should be less rude. We are standing next to a freeway. You wouldn't want Mr Maclean to push you in front of a moving car.'

'All right, I'll explain,' said Friday. 'The bus was travelling at one hundred kilometres per hour. It never turned, accelerated or decelerated. Therefore, the hair would not have moved. The hair sitting on the bus floor had the same momentum as the bus. It's only when the bus changes its movement, that the hair would change its position. Therefore the location of the hair is proof.'

'I'm going to call the Headmaster,' said Mr Maclean, taking out his mobile phone.

'Sir,' said Friday, 'don't be too hasty. If you inform the Headmaster, he will have to suspend them. This is a serious breach of school rules.'

'Too right,' agreed Mr Maclean, starting to dial.

'But think about it,' urged Friday. 'Getting suspended from a camp in the wilderness – nothing could delight them more. They'd love to go home to their computers and lovely clothes.'

Mr Maclean glanced up at the girls in question. They were looking unbelievably smug.

'That's probably the whole reason they came up with this ridiculous prank,' said Friday. 'If you really want to punish them, I've got a far better idea.'

'What?' asked Mr Maclean.

'Make them change the tyre on the bus,' said Friday.

What followed was a wonderful hour of entertainment. Everyone got out of the bus and watched as the five girls changed the tyre while the bus driver gave them instructions. Watching them try to use tools, move a filthy tyre and work as a team was pricelessly funny. Even Mr Maclean had a good laugh. The best bit was when Trea Babcock slipped over in a muddy puddle and the spare tyre rolled right over her.

By the time they got back on the bus everyone was in a buoyant mood, ready for their adventure ahead. Except for the five culprits, who were now plotting ways of taking revenge on Friday.

Chapter 9

▰▰▰▰▰▰▰▰▰▰▰▰▰

Arrival

As the bus pulled in through the gates of Camp Courage, the students were very cheerful. This was largely due to the fact that for the first time in four hours they were going to be allowed to use the lavatory. But some students were excited just to be away from their desks and textbooks. Friday was not so upbeat.

'This camp is surprisingly scruffy,' said Friday as she looked about at the location. There was one building that was a regular timber house, and alongside it was a larger building with the words 'Mess Hall' handpainted on a plank of wood nailed to the front doorway. Both buildings looked like they hadn't been painted in fifty years. The bus pulled up in the central dirt courtyard, next to a sports field covered in dried-out yellow grass.

'I wouldn't have thought you'd mind a scruffy building,' said Melanie. 'You seem to like most other scruffy things.'

'I don't,' said Friday. 'I just think it's odd. Highcrest is such a fancy school, I'd assumed they'd be sending us to a fancy camp as well.'

'They didn't have much choice,' said Melanie. 'This is the first time they've been able to hold the camp in five years. The school has been banned from all the reputable camps within a five hundred-kilometre radius.'

'Why?' asked Friday.

'My family is partly to blame,' said Melanie.

'Really?' said Friday. She only knew Melanie and her older brother Binky, and they were both lovely and totally harmless.

'Five years ago my older brother Jub . . .' began Melanie.

'Hold it right there,' said Friday. 'You have a brother called Jub?'

'Hey, your siblings are called Halley, Orion, Quasar and Kryptonite,' said Melanie.

'*Quantum*,' corrected Friday. 'Although if my mother ever does have a sixth child, I will suggest "Kryptonite" to her.'

'Anyway, Jub fell asleep and accidentally set fire to his hut,' said Melanie.

'How do you start a fire when you're sleeping?' asked Friday.

'He was cooking pizza on an open fire,' said Melanie.

'Okay, I can imagine that,' said Friday.

'And the year before that, my other brother Henk,' continued Melanie, 'tried surfing a bore wave up a river and ended up twenty kilometres from camp. It took him three days to walk back.'

'So your family have been systematically ruining camps for years,' said Friday.

'The year before that it wasn't any of my brothers,' said Melanie. 'One of the supervising teachers couldn't handle the pressure. He went mad and blew up the mess hall.'

'Why?' asked Friday.

'He didn't like the food,' said Melanie. 'Once you've had Mrs Marigold's cooking, baked beans every day just doesn't cut it.'

'Line up, maggots!'

Friday and Melanie turned around to see a rotund middle-aged woman standing on the verandah of the mess hall. She was dressed in khaki shorts and shirt, thick leather boots and a large broad brim hat, as if she was going on an African safari and needed to be ready to run away from lions. But the most eye-catching thing about this woman was that she had a prosthetic leg. Her left leg from the knee down was made of plastic and aluminium. No attempt had been made to paint the leg; it was the colour of the original materials.

'Did she just call us maggots?' asked Friday.

'Move your butts!' yelled the lady even louder. 'Two straight lines. Right now. On the double!'

The students started to shuffle in the direction she had indicated. Highcrest Academy students did not often have to line up. Their school had given up most attempts at trying to instil order on the student body, so forming lines was an alien thing to them.

'Everybody freeze!' screamed the woman. She sounded so genuinely angry that even the most disrespectful students froze where they were. 'You stuck-up rich kids are pathetic! You can't even form two lines when you're told to.'

'I don't think this lady has heard about positive reinforcement and building self-esteem,' Melanie whispered to Friday.

'Drop and give me twenty!' hollered the woman.

'Twenty what?' asked Friday. Having grown up in a house full of physicists, Friday had not watched the usual war movies and was not familiar with the expression.

'Now!' bellowed the woman. And so great was her natural authority that all the students did get down on their hands and knees and start doing push-ups.

'Bravo!' said Mr Maclean. 'It's about time someone showed these children who's in charge.'

The woman turned and glared at Mr Maclean. She took in his polished boat shoes, immaculate chinos and freshly ironed shirt. 'You can drop and give me twenty as well!'

'But I'm a teacher,' blustered Mr Maclean.

'I'm in charge here,' yelled the woman, 'and I say, DROP AND GIVE ME TWENTY!'

Mr Maclean was face down on the ground knocking out push-ups before the echo of her yell had stopped reverberating off the buildings.

Everyone was doing push-ups now. Even Melanie. And it was particularly hard for her because she had no upper-body strength.

'My name is Geraldine and I am in charge of you for the next four weeks,' she bellowed. 'You aren't at your posh school or your fancypants homes now. You're in my world. And my world is your worst nightmare!'

'There are so many contradictions in the collection of metaphors she has just used,' whispered Friday between push-ups.

'Huh,' said Melanie. She wasn't capable of more advanced speech because she was so exhausted.

'You may not want to be here,' said Geraldine. 'Tough. I don't care. I don't want to be here taking care of you lot, either. But we're stuck with each other and the only way you're going to make it through is by following the rules. Rule one – do as you're told! Rule two – never *ever* ask me about my leg.

Rule three – and this is the most important one – do not go near the river at night! That's when the ghost of Ghost Mountain comes down from the hills in search of children to torment.'

'Oh, please,' said Friday, pausing mid push-up and kneeling up. 'I enjoy hyperbole and storytelling as much as the next person –'

'No, you don't,' panted Melanie.

'But a ghost?' said Friday. 'You can't expect us to believe in that.'

'I don't care what you believe,' said Geraldine. 'I just don't want to have to fill out the paperwork when the ghost drowns you in the river. Now, hurry up! The first ten people to finish their push-ups are going to win a prize.'

The more athletic students started push-upping faster. The first few finished and ran out to the front. Ian was amongst them. Then Jessica Dawes and Mirabella Peterson leapt up and raced forward. Soon the ten spots were full.

Everyone else slowed down again.

'You ten get the best accommodation,' announced Geraldine.

The athletic students cheered.

'You get the Treehouse,' said Geraldine. 'You'll be competing against the other teams to gain privileges and avoid penalties. Pedro is your counsellor.'

A swarthy man stepped forward. He looked more like a professional boxer than a camp counsellor. He was wearing khaki like Geraldine, but with long sleeves and trousers. From the number of tattoos visible above the neckline of his shirt, Friday guessed he most likely would have a lot of tattoos on his arms and legs as well. Perhaps with some rude language that needed to be covered in front of children.

'This way,' said Pedro. He turned and walked into the forest. The Treehouse team nervously followed him.

'You don't think he's taking them off to kill them, do you?' asked Friday.

'They get all the luck,' said Melanie.

Another ten students had finished and straggled to the front.

'You ten get the next best accommodation,' announced Geraldine. 'You're in the Tent with Nadia.'

'If a tent is second best,' whispered Melanie, between her eleventh and twelfth push-ups, 'how bad are third and fourth going to be?'

A muscular blonde woman stepped forward. She was very good-looking, although she had a lot of nasty scratches on her forearms.

'I wonder how she got those scratches,' said Friday.

'There must be a lot of thorny bushes near the Tent,' said Melanie.

The Tent team followed Nadia into the forest.

Another ten students had finished and gathered at the front.

'You are pathetic,' said Geraldine. 'But at least you're not as pathetic as that lot.' She pointed at the least athletic students. There were only six of them still doing push-ups.

'You ten get the Hole,' said Geraldine. 'Go with Louise.'

Louise stepped forward. She was in her mid-twenties too. She had red hair tied back in long dreadlocks. She beckoned to her group and they began following her up the road towards the Hole.

By the time Friday finished and looked around, it was to see that she actually wasn't last. Rajiv Patel had sprained his wrist playing Dungeons and Dragons (trying to put too much spin on the dice), so he was still struggling with one-handed push-ups. And Susan Baines was still going. She had asthma and had already stopped twice to take puffs from her ventolin inhaler.

Friday and Patel joined Melanie, Digby Harvey, a large short-sighted boy, and Wai-Yi Yap, a girl who was almost as much a bookworm as Friday. They all watched Susan struggle through her last couple of reps.

'So you lot are the losers,' said Geraldine, taking the time to glare hatefully into the eyes of each and every student individually. 'You make me sick. I'm not going to put up with it. I've got four weeks to whip you into shape. And that's going to happen. Do I make myself clear?'

Friday took a breath about to speak, but Melanie stomped hard on her foot.

'Ow!' cried Friday.

'What was that?' snapped Geraldine.

'Nothing,' said Melanie. 'She just got bitten by a spider.'

'Good,' said Geraldine. 'It will toughen her up. You ten are in the worst accommodation.'

'But there are only six of us,' said Wai-Yi.

'I was told there would be forty students, so if four of them didn't turn up, that's not my fault,' said Geraldine.

'They must be the smartest four,' muttered Susan.

'But if we're competing against the other teams, it won't be fair,' said Harvey.

'Life isn't fair,' said Geraldine, 'especially for losers. You lot need to toughen up and get used to it. You're in the Houseboat down on the river.'

'Didn't you just say there was a ghost down by the river?' asked Susan.

'Yes, that's why it's the worst accommodation,' said Geraldine. 'Now get out of my sight!'

The six students looked about, but there was no counsellor for them to follow.

'Where's our counsellor?' asked Friday.

'What did you say?' demanded Geraldine. Turning around, she marched right up to Friday and stood so uncomfortably close that Friday had to lean backwards.

'The other groups had counsellors to show them to their accommodation,' said Friday, 'I assumed we'd get a counsellor too.'

'You assumed, did you?' said Geraldine. 'Well, this is a wilderness survival camp. Don't assume anything. What would you do if your counsellor got eaten by a bear?'

'I'd probably be traumatised and seek psychiatric counselling,' said Melanie.

'I'd run away from the bear,' said Patel.

'You'd get on with it and cope on your own!' yelled Geraldine. 'So you can practise now – you can find the Houseboat yourself. Or your counsellor. Whichever one you come across first.' She stalked off.

'Is it too late to go home?' asked Susan.

Friday turned and looked up the road. The bus was long gone. 'I'm afraid so.'

'How are we going to find the Houseboat?' asked Harvey. He was wearing very thick glasses. His eyesight clearly wasn't good.

'Well, if it's a houseboat and it's on the river, then it must be downhill,' said Friday. 'Let's see.'

Chapter 10

Sebastian

The Houseboat was even more underwhelming than the rest of the camp. The word 'houseboat' had evocative romantic connotations of lazy afternoons drifting along a serene river, revelling in the beauty of nature. In reality, this houseboat was just a floating shack.

'Why a houseboat?' wondered Susan. 'At least in a regular shack, if it collapses, you just get a head injury. With this, when it collapses, we'll all drown.'

'They probably use it because it's cheaper than constructing a building with proper foundations,' said Friday.

'And you wouldn't need to get planning permission,' said Harvey. 'My dad is in development. Planning permission is always the hardest part of any job.'

'Maybe it's nicer inside,' said Melanie.

They all trooped aboard to see for themselves.

It was not nicer inside. There were three bedrooms, but none of the furniture you would normally associate with a bedroom, just mattresses lying on the floor. Between the bedrooms was a common room with two very decrepit old couches, and a shelf holding some drinking glasses and an ancient stereo.

'It looks like the inside of one of those shipping containers you see on the news that's been used to smuggle illegal immigrants across a border,' said Patel.

'Is that how your family came to this country?' asked Harvey.

'My family arrived one hundred and twenty years ago on a luxury cruise liner they owned themselves,' said Patel.

'What's that sound?' asked Friday.

The group stopped to listen. It was surprisingly noisy on the river in the middle of the forest. There was the lapping of the water, the squawking of birds and the wind in the trees. But above it all, they could hear a faint droning.

'It sounds like someone snoring,' said Melanie.

'It's coming from the back of the boat,' said Friday. 'Let's investigate.'

They went out on deck. There was a narrow walkway around the outside of the boat, which they followed to the back, or stern, as they say in nautical circles, where there was a narrow steep staircase.

'It must be someone on the roof,' said Friday.

'Maybe it's a home invader!' said Wai-Yi.

'Why would they break in then take a nap?' asked Friday.

'It's the type of thing I'd do,' said Melanie.

Friday took to the stairs first. She crept up, just in case this was the world's weirdest home invasion. When she poked her head out above the flat roof of the Houseboat she was relieved to see no one. There was a small shed towards the front of the boat.

'That must be the wheelhouse,' said Friday. 'The captain would steer the boat from there.'

'That's where the noise is coming from,' said Harvey.

They walked across the roof to the shed. There were windows on all four sides so the captain could see in every direction. Friday and the others peered in.

Inside was a steering wheel and the controls for operating the Houseboat. But they were so covered in dust that they didn't look like they'd been used for some time. Now it was a bedroom. Dirty clothes and toiletries were strewn about, and in the limited amount of floor space a mattress had been squeezed in. And sprawled across it was a large, lanky man. He was fast asleep and snoring.

'This is how the three bears must have felt when they came back to find Goldilocks in their bed,' said Melanie.

'Is he some kind of vagrant?' asked Harvey.

'I know who he is,' said Friday.

'He's not one of your physicist relatives, is he?' asked Melanie.

'Why do you say that?' asked Friday.

'He's scruffy enough,' said Melanie.

'My relatives may be messy, absentminded and bad at ironing clothes,' said Friday, 'but they would never dream of living on a houseboat.'

Friday stepped across to the cabin door and knocked. The man lying on the bed sat up with a jolt. When he looked around and saw six children staring at him through the window he yelped in shock. 'Agh! What are you doing here?!'

Friday opened the door. 'Hello, my name is Friday Barnes. I take it you're Sebastian St John?'

'How did you know that?' asked Sebastian suspiciously.

'The bag hanging on the hook behind your head has a name tag on it,' said Friday. 'From the Camp Courage t-shirt on the floor, I take it you are our camp counsellor.'

'Yes,' said Sebastian, hurriedly putting on his t-shirt. 'You're early.'

'No,' said Friday, '*you're* late. Or rather, you were absent. To say you were late would imply that you had actually turned up to our arrival. Which you clearly did not.'

'Friday, you might want to tone it back,' said Melanie. 'Waking someone up is never a good first impression. You don't want your second, third and fourth impressions to be bad too.'

'We were allocated the Houseboat as our dorm,' said Harvey.

'Bad at push-ups, were you?' said Sebastian with a sigh. 'I always get the ones who are bad at push-ups. But the main thing is – can you all swim?'

Everyone in the group nodded.

'Not terribly well,' admitted Friday.

'Pretty badly, in fact,' said Susan.

'Then don't fall overboard,' said Sebastian. 'There's a waterfall downstream. If you have a history of sleepwalking, you might want to tie your ankle to the bedframe before you go to bed at night. And whatever happens, once it's dark outside, stay inside the Houseboat.'

'Why?' asked Harvey.

'Because of the ghost,' said Sebastian.

'Not you too?' said Friday. 'You can't really expect us to believe something so silly.'

'Plenty of campers claim to have seen it,' said Sebastian, 'and it's just a fact that anyone who wanders around at night ends up having mysterious accidents.'

'Probably because it's dark and they bump into things,' said Friday.

'Who is the ghost a ghost of?' asked Susan. 'I mean, who were they when they were alive?'

'They say it's the ghost of a former counsellor,' said Sebastian. 'One of his campers fell into the river just after a storm when the water was high. The counsellor dived in to save the camper, but as he was pulling the kid out of the water, a log washed downstream and hit him in the back of the head. His body was swept away and they never found it.'

'What happened to the kid?' asked Melanie.

'She scrambled to shore,' said Sebastian. 'She survived, but broke her leg badly when she fell in. It became infected in the stormwater and had to be amputated.'

'Are you saying . . . it was Geraldine?' asked Wai-Yi.

Sebastian nodded.

'That's farcical,' said Friday. 'Geraldine can't be more than fifty years old. Penicillin has been readily available her entire lifetime.'

'The doctors said it was blood poisoning,' said Sebastian. 'There was nothing they could do. But legend has it that the ghost put a curse on her.'

'Is that why she couldn't get a proper job and had to work at the place of her horrific childhood accident?' asked Melanie.

'I don't know,' said Sebastian. 'It all happened long before my time. I just know you should stay in here where it's safe at night. Come on, I'd better show you around.'

Sebastian split them up so the boys got the biggest bedroom. This was no disappointment to Friday. The extra space was somewhat nullified by the huge growth of black mould across one of the walls. Meanwhile, the girls were separated into the two bedrooms on the far side of the common room. Friday would be sharing with Melanie, which was a relief to both of them because they were used to each other's eccentricities. Wai-Yi and Susan were in the other.

'So this is home for the next four weeks,' said Friday as she sat down on her slightly damp mattress.

'I like it,' said Melanie.

'You do?' asked Friday.

'I've got a room with a mattress and no maths lessons for four weeks,' said Melanie. 'It's lovely.'

'But don't you think it's all a bit weird?' said Friday. 'An irrationally angry amputee, and facilities that don't appear to comply with any known building code?'

'We're supposed to be learning survival skills,' said Melanie. 'They obviously take that seriously.'

'And a counsellor who doesn't even turn up to the introductory session because he's too busy sleeping?' said Friday. 'Doesn't that strike you as suspicious?'

'It strikes me as the most sensible thing I've seen since I got here,' said Melanie.

'But the most mysterious thing is this crazy story about the ghost,' said Friday. 'There's something weird going on here.'

'Remember your promise to the Headmaster?' said Melanie. 'Even if there is something weird going on, you promised you wouldn't do anything about it.'

'Hmm,' said Friday, but she wasn't really listening to her friend. Her mind was too busy ticking over.

Chapter 11

~~~~~~~~~~~~~~~~~~~~~~~~~

Fire Alarm

The first week at Camp Courage was more awful than Friday had expected. It was the mundanity that was so disappointing. Friday did not enjoy 'extreme sports', but she appreciated the importance of learning new skills, so she'd looked forward to rock climbing, raft building and flying-fox rides. Camp Courage had nothing like that. There was just a lot of woodchopping, water fetching and building repair. They didn't even get to eat wilderness food.

Friday had imagined they would be fishing and learning what berries and leaves they could eat. But all the meals were the dreadful type of processed, high-fat, high-preservative, overcooked slop that you usually only got in prisons, hospitals and inflight meals.

Having no common sense when it came to social interaction, Friday was silly enough to ask Geraldine about it.

'Are we going to learn any wilderness survival skills at this camp?' asked Friday. 'So far our team has chopped three cubic metres of wood, fetched several hundreds of buckets of water to the kitchen, and spent two days redoing the bitumen tile roof on the Houseboat.'

'Those are survival skills,' snapped Geraldine. 'You need wood to make fire, water to drink, and shelter so you don't freeze to death.'

'Yes, but it's hardly bushcraft, is it?' said Friday.

'Excuse me if the actual practical wilderness survival skills you've been learning aren't up to your high standards,' said Geraldine sarcastically. 'It's not all drinking-your-own-urine, you know. What do you want me to do? Put on a bear for you to wrestle?'

'Shouldn't we be learning how to light a fire?' asked Friday.

'You're not ready for fire!' barked Geraldine. 'I've seen you try to chop wood. A newborn baby would be better at it than you.'

'Really?' said Melanie. 'I would have thought there were laws preventing you from giving a newborn baby an axe. And mothers preventing you as well.'

'Fire-making skills are a privilege!' yelled Geraldine. 'You need to work on your rudimentary not-dying skills first.'

'And another thing,' said Friday, 'this story about a ghost is scaring people. Do you want me to investigate and find out what's going on? I'd be willing to accept payment in the form of not having to chop any more wood.'

'I forbid you to do that!' bellowed Geraldine. 'I like running a haunted camp. Fear of the undead is the only thing that keeps you brats in bed at night. I just wish the ghost would push more of you into the river!'

Geraldine stomped off.

When Friday returned to the Houseboat after dinner that night, the group found another five tonnes of firewood for them to chop up.

'Thanks, Friday,' said Patel.

'It's not my fault,' said Friday. 'I was just questioning her syllabus choices and offering to debunk the camp's mythology.'

'When you say that,' said Wai-Yi, 'can you hear how annoying you sound?'

'You're lucky she only gave us wood to chop,' said Harvey. 'I bet she would have loved to have thrown you in the river.'

'I don't understand why we're basically doing maintenance tasks,' said Friday, 'and why Geraldine is yelling at us all the time. Her anger seems to be totally disproportional to anything we've actually done.'

'You'd probably be grumpy too if your leg had been bitten off by a bear,' said Melanie.

'What?' said Friday.

'That's how she lost her leg,' said Melanie.

'But what about the story Sebastian told us?' said Friday.

'Maybe he made it up,' said Melanie. 'I heard she was in Alaska working on the gas pipeline when she was attacked by a bear.'

'Really?' said Wai-Yi. 'I heard she fell off a boat on the Amazon River and it was eaten off by piranhas.'

'No, the way I heard it,' said Harvey, 'was that she was in the army doing night-ops when a tank ran over her foot.'

'That's ridiculous,' said Friday.

'Which one?' asked Melanie.

'All of them,' said Friday. 'If you're attacked by a bear they always go for the back of your neck, not your lower leg. Geraldine would have disfiguring face and neck scars.'

'Perhaps she has a really good plastic surgeon?' said Susan.

'And piranhas wouldn't eat your foot,' said Friday. 'Anyone travelling in the Amazon would be wearing boots. A piranha isn't going to eat through your boot when it could go for the soft flesh of your face and eyeballs first.'

'What about the tank story?' asked Patel. 'That sounds pretty believable to me. She yells at everyone like a drill sergeant.'

'No, that can't be right,' said Friday. 'Geraldine has clearly not been in the military. It's forty years since drill sergeants were allowed to yell at people like that. These days they can't say anything disparaging or derogatory, or they'll end up in front of a disciplinary hearing.'

'Then how do you think she lost her leg?' asked Melanie.

'It's a mystery,' said Friday. 'I would need more clues to figure it out.'

'We could just ask her,' said Melanie.

'If you did that,' said Friday, 'my next case would be the mystery of the missing Melanie.'

They say that fresh air makes you sleep like a log. That is certainly true. Especially if you spend your time in the fresh air chopping wood, scraping lichen off roofs and digging holes. After a particularly long day of scrubbing the mess hall, inside and out, Friday fell into a deep slumber as soon as her head hit the pillow. For once her brain didn't set to work on complicated problems the moment her eyes shut. She just fell, like an anvil out of a window onto a cartoon character's head, into a deep sleep.

BEEP BEEP BEEP BEEP BEEP!

Friday was having a horrible dream about being trapped in a fire, but that wasn't what upset her. She was annoyed because, in the dream, she was trying to do her maths homework and couldn't concentrate with the smoke alarm going off. As Friday's brain slowly clawed its way to consciousness, she became aware that the noise she was hearing was not part of the dream – there really was a smoke alarm going off, just as another part of her brain noticed that she could smell smoke!

'Get up, get up!' screamed Friday. She ran over to Melanie's bed and shook her friend.

'Huh,' mumbled Melanie, trying to snuggle deeper under her blanket.

'The Houseboat is on fire!' said Friday.

'Good, I'm cold,' said Melanie.

Friday ran to the doorway of the other girls' room. Susan and Wai-Yi were already up and hurrying to put their shoes on. Melanie still hadn't moved.

'Susan, you go and make sure the boys are up,' said Friday. 'Wai-Yi, help me get Melanie out of bed.'

Wai-Yi came over. 'How?' she asked.

Friday looked at Melanie. It was going to be hard to shift her.

'Grab a corner of the sheet,' said Friday. 'We'll drag her.'

Friday grabbed one corner while Wai-Yi grabbed another and they started to pull. They got Melanie off the bed easily enough, although she hit the ground with quite a thud. Then they hurriedly dragged her into the common room. The smoke was thicker here.

'Stay down low,' urged Friday. 'Smoke rises. The air is clearer down low.'

The two girls crouched and pulled Melanie towards the boat's gangplank, coughing and spluttering as they went. It was a relief to get her out the door and be able to breathe fresh air again.

When Melanie was safely on the bank, and they did a headcount making sure all six of them were there, the Houseboat team collapsed on the ground to catch their breaths. Melanie's eyes fluttered open and she sat up.

'Did I go to sleep out here?' she asked. 'I thought we were staying on a houseboat.'

'There's a fire,' said Friday. 'We had to evacuate.'

'Really?' said Melanie. She turned to look at the Houseboat.

The smoke had eased, and there was only a small trickle coming out of the window.

'Where's the fire?' asked Melanie.

Friday looked at the boat and realised there was no sign of one. 'I didn't see the actual fire. Was it in the boys' room?'

Patel and Harvey shook their heads.

'No, there was smoke, but the fire wasn't in our room,' said Patel.

'The fire must have put itself out,' said Susan.

'It doesn't make any sense,' said Friday. 'That houseboat is a deathtrap. It's made of rotten old timber, and filled with highly flammable cheap mattresses and no doubt dodgy electrical wiring. If there were a fire, the whole thing should be ablaze by now.'

Suddenly the bank was floodlit. Friday held up a hand as she was blinded by the light.

'Aagghhh!' screamed Susan. 'It's the ghost of Ghost Mountain, come to kill us all!'

'Be quiet, girl!'

'That doesn't sound like a ghost,' said Melanie. 'It sounds like Geraldine.'

Their eyes adjusted to the light and they could see that it was, indeed, their formidable leader.

'Caught red-handed!' cried Geraldine.

'What?' asked Friday.

'Breaking curfew!' accused Geraldine. 'And stealing food!'

Geraldine swung her flashlight across the clearing where a large pile of snack food was sitting on the grass beneath a tree.

'We didn't put that there!' cried Friday.

'Hah!' said Geraldine. 'That's what all you hoodlums say.'

'We only came out here because there was a fire,' said Friday.

'Where?' demanded Geraldine. 'I can't see a fire.'

'There isn't one anymore,' said Melanie.

'But the fire alarm went off so we evacuated,' said Friday.

'Aha!' said Geraldine. 'Caught in your own web of lies. I know for a fact that isn't true, because the Houseboat doesn't have a smoke alarm. None of the dormitories do.'

'Is that legal?' asked Patel.

'Potato-peeling duty for you!' declared Geraldine. Patel slumped. 'This is a camp. And tents don't need to have smoke alarms.'

'But the Houseboat isn't a tent,' said Friday.

'Don't argue with me,' said Geraldine. 'The same rules apply.'

'So can we go back to bed then?' asked Melanie with a yawn.

'You cannot,' said Geraldine. 'As punishment for stealing food, you get nothing but bread and water for three days.'

'Now that definitely isn't legal,' said Susan. 'You can't starve children.'

'Of course I can,' said Geraldine. 'This is a survival skills camp. If you want to supplement your diet, all you have to do is catch or harvest your meals from the wilderness.'

'I knew I should have read a book about fishing before we went away,' said Friday.

'There'll be no time for that,' said Geraldine, 'because your other punishment for breaking curfew is digging the new latrine.'

'But the latrines here are connected to the sewerage system,' said Friday. 'They're proper flushing toilets.'

'Latrine digging is an important survival skill,' said Geraldine. 'You need to learn how to do it if you're going to be self-sufficient in the wilderness.'

The six students groaned.

'Now get to bed,' ordered Geraldine. 'You start digging at first light.'

'No, wait,' said Friday. 'There was definitely a smoke alarm and smoke. We all heard and smelled it. We should investigate.'

'Oh, please,' said Geraldine. 'This isn't some public service bureaucracy where we investigate and analyse everything. It's a camp. You've been caught sneaking around after lights off. When I say "Go back to bed", you go back to bed. That's it. Case closed.'

'What if we can prove there was a fire?' said Friday.

'Or what if there actually is a fire?' said Melanie. 'It could be slowly smouldering away. Fires do that, you know. My great grandmother set fire to her house once when she fell asleep while eating toasted marshmallows in bed. The embers on the marshmallows smouldered for hours before the sheets caught fire. Luckily she'd drunk an enormous amount of iced tea that day, so she was in the bathroom when the flames flared up.'

'You see, there's precedent,' said Friday. 'We need to check this out.'

'Fine, show me this fire then,' said Geraldine. 'But if you can't produce one, you get double latrine duty.'

'What's double latrine duty?' asked Patel.

'You dig latrines, and then you fill them in. And when that's done, you dig them out again,' said Geraldine. 'It's character-building.'

Geraldine marched up the gangplank and the others followed. The Houseboat seemed even more flimsy with her heavily stomping around the deck. She stepped into the common room and switched on the light.

'I don't see any fire,' said Geraldine.

Friday and the other students looked about. There was no sign of fire. There wasn't even any indication of smoke, just an unpleasant chemical odour in the air.

'The smoke must have come from somewhere,' said Friday, glancing about the room.

'I ought to add to your punishment,' said Geraldine. 'Look at this mess!' She kicked a piece of aluminium foil on the ground.

'What is that?' asked Friday, bending down to pick it up.

'No doubt a wrapper from some of the food you've stolen,' said Geraldine.

Friday inspected the foil closely. It was very scrunched up. There was a long thin piece with a circle at one end. Friday sniffed it.

'What are you doing?' snapped Geraldine.

'Don't take it personally,' said Melanie. 'She sniffs everything.'

The other students nodded. They had seen Friday sniff much stranger things many times before.

'It smells of plastic,' said Friday. 'Burned plastic.'

'We don't put burned plastic in any of the food here,' said Geraldine. 'At least, not intentionally. Occasionally something will drop in, but there's nothing we can do about that.'

Friday unwrapped the foil. The long thin bit was empty, just several layers of foil, but the larger circle held something inside.

'What is that?' asked Melanie.

'It looks like a black and orange blob,' said Patel, peering over Friday's shoulder.

'The black is burn marks,' said Friday. 'And the orange is the original colour of the plastic.' She sniffed it again. 'This is a smoke bomb!'

'What?' demanded Geraldine. 'This isn't a war zone. It's a camp for children, teaching them healthy outdoor pursuits.'

'What's so healthy about rationed food and digging latrines?' asked Melanie.

'It teaches you a lesson about having a smart mouth,' said Geraldine.

'Have any of the ping-pong balls from the rec room gone missing recently?' asked Friday.

Geraldine flinched in shock. 'How did you know about that? It was only reported to me this afternoon.'

'This orange plastic is the distinctive colour of ping-pong balls,' said Friday. 'You can make a smoke bomb out of them. I'm not going to explain how, in case any of the boys here get ideas.' Friday glared at Patel.

'Why are you looking at me?' asked Patel defensively.

'The plastic burns slowly and releases a dark smoke,' said Friday. 'The foil would be shaped to slowly release it, without setting fire to the Houseboat.'

'Ridiculous,' said Geraldine.

'And that smoke would have tripped the smoke alarm,' said Friday.

'But there are no smoke alarms,' said Geraldine. 'I saw to that myself. Nasty modern things that always beep when the battery starts to go.'

'But we all heard an alarm go off, didn't we?' asked Friday.

'I didn't,' said Melanie unhelpfully.

Friday looked about. There were no smoke alarms on the ceilings or walls in any of the three rooms.

'The alarm must have come from somewhere,' said Friday. She walked over to the stereo. It was a very old one from the eighties with a double tape deck and a graphic equaliser. 'There's a tape in here. Did anyone bring a tape from home?'

The students all shook their heads.

Friday rewound the tape to the beginning and pressed play. Suddenly the air was split by the deafening sound of a smoke alarm.

'Turn that off!' screamed Geraldine.

Friday complied. 'Someone put this recording of a smoke alarm in here?' she asked.

'Who on earth would want to do that?' said Geraldine. 'This is ridiculous.'

'There are quite a lot of people, actually,' said Melanie. 'Most people don't like Friday very much.

The five girls she got in trouble on the bus ride down here, in particular.'

'But how could they have made this recording?' asked Patel.

'Do all the huts have stereos?' asked Friday.

'Yes,' said Geraldine. 'We use them for playing Wagnerian opera first thing in the morning when we want to wake the students up early.'

'So all they would need is a tape and a smoke alarm to make a recording,' said Friday. 'There's definitely a smoke alarm in the mess hall. They could have taken it down and used that.'

'But who would do something like this?' asked Wai-Yi.

'Aha!' cried Friday before throwing herself on the ground and reaching right under the coffee table.

'Is she having some sort of fit?' asked Geraldine.

'No, I'm collecting evidence,' said Friday. She pulled herself out from under the coffee table. 'Behold – a false eyelash!'

'So?' said Geraldine.

'There's only one person here at camp wearing false eyelashes,' said Friday. 'Mirabella Peterson.'

'But you helped her on the bus,' said Susan. 'You proved who cut her hair.'

'That's why she would have to do this,' said Friday. 'To gain readmission to her group of friends, she would have to play a cruel prank distancing herself from me.'

Suddenly, Sebastian stumbled in through the front door.

'What's going on?' he asked.

'Where have you been?' demanded Geraldine. She sniffed. 'You stink of poop.'

'Have you been digging latrines?' asked Melanie.

'I don't think Geraldine is allowed to punish counsellors as well,' said Susan.

'I don't see why not,' said Melanie. 'They're not terribly good at their job. We can't find Sebastian half the time. The other half he's in his bedroom sleeping. And all the counsellors seem to regularly fall into thorny bushes.'

'I heard a noise in the forest,' said Sebastian, 'so I went to investigate.'

'It was probably our prankster,' said Friday.

'How did you get so messy?' asked Geraldine.

Sebastian's hands and knees were filthy.

'I tripped over a tree root and fell,' said Sebastian. 'I must have stumbled on some animal droppings.'

'Scat,' said Friday.

'What?' said Sebastian.

'Animal droppings are called scat by hunters and wildness survival experts,' said Friday. 'You should know that.'

'It smells like you fell over a lot of tree roots,' said Melanie.

'Did you fall in the river too?' asked Friday. 'Your boots are wet.'

Everyone looked at Sebastian's feet. They were saturated. And he had tramped muddy footprints into the room.

'Potato-peeling duty for you for a week!' snapped Sebastian.

'What?' asked Friday. 'What did I do?'

'You're too nosey for your own good,' said Sebastian.

'He's got a point,' said Melanie.

'I've already given them latrine duty,' said Geraldine.

'You can't give us latrine duty,' said Friday. 'I proved we were set up with a smoke bomb and a fake fire alarm.'

'Unless you set all that up as a cover for the stolen food outside,' said Geraldine.

'I'm not that hungry,' said Friday.

'I am,' said Harvey. 'I'll take the punishment if we get to keep the food.'

'You don't get the food,' said Geraldine. 'But you do get the punishment for wasting my time.'

'That's totally unfair,' said Friday.

'Good,' said Geraldine. 'Life is unfair. I'm teaching you a valuable lesson.' She stalked away.

'Get back to bed,' snapped Sebastian before going to his own room and slamming the door shut.

'I suppose we might as well,' said Friday, turning to her own room, only to find Melanie fast asleep in bed already.

The others were settling down too. But Friday was too full of adrenalin to go to sleep straight away, and too puzzled by the irrationality of Sebastian and Geraldine. She stepped outside onto the deck of the Houseboat, leaned on the railing and looked up at the stars. In the northern sky she could see Orion. It seemed like a lifetime ago they had been following that constellation to find Ian.

Just then, Friday noticed a movement out of the corner of her eye. She glanced across to the far side of the river.

Something was moving along the riverbank. It was a glowing green human shape.

Friday rubbed her eyes and blinked several times. Her eyesight wasn't very good. Perhaps the darkness and the blinding floodlight was making her see things. She looked again and the shape was definitely still there. It was moving away through the trees now, disappearing from view.

'I must be imagining things,' muttered Friday, shaking her head. 'Ghosts aren't real.'

Chapter 12

River Challenge

Over the next week the Houseboat team dug the latrines and peeled the potatoes, and continued on with the monotony of the camp. The counsellors had started taking it in turns leading all the students on long bushwalks every day. Friday suspected this was so the other three counsellors could hang around at the camp doing nothing. They seemed to spend more time napping than Melanie. Nadia, Louise, Pedro and Sebastian seemed very random choices for their jobs. None of them showed any interest in nature or wilderness skills, so the long hikes weren't even punctuated with fun facts about botany or camping tips. Between the walking, the tedious lessons and the endless chores, Camp Courage was proving to be exhausting. One of the least pleasant things about it was the way the students were woken up every morning.

Ride of the Valkyries was still blasting as Friday, Melanie and the rest of the Houseboat team made their way up to the mess hall.

'Is it me or are they waking us up even earlier than usual?' asked Melanie with a yawn.

'It's earlier,' said Friday.

'Really? How can you know for sure?' asked Melanie.

'It's still dark,' said Friday.

Melanie looked up at the black sky. 'Good heavens, you're right. These people are even more dementedly cruel than I realised.'

As they arrived at the dining hall, the girls could see that there was a crowd gathered outside.

'That's odd,' said Friday. Usually people went straight in and began eating.

'What's happening?' Friday asked the first person she came to at the back of the crowd. But that first person was Mirabella Peterson. Friday didn't recognise her immediately. She had never seen Mirabella not wearing false eyelashes before. Mirabella looked Friday up and down, then turned away with a sniff of distain.

Friday rolled her eyes. It was too early in the morning for petty social politics. She pushed her way through the crowd so she could see for herself.

There was a sign on the mess hall door saying, 'Closed.'

'Do you think they've decided to save money on food by starving us all to death?' asked Melanie.

'I doubt it,' said Friday. 'It would be a false economy. Then they'd have to pay out all the lawsuits to the annoyed parents.'

'Good morning, maggots!'

Geraldine was standing at the back of the group, addressing them.

'Hungry, are you?' asked Geraldine.

From the gleeful glint in her eye, the students could tell that something deeply unpleasant was about to be laid out.

'Well, I know you are all such toffy, fancy ladies and gents, so today we've decided to give you a little surprise. Today, we're going to be serving breakfast down by the river.'

'That sounds nice,' said Melanie.

'It's not going to be nice,' said Friday. 'There's going to be a catch.'

'The only thing is,' said Geraldine, 'the food is all on the far side of the river.'

Everyone groaned.

Geraldine smirked. 'And there are four huts, but only three packages of food. One hut will miss out.'

The Treehouse members sniggered and looked across at the ragtag group of Houseboaters.

'Who gets the food will be decided by who grabs it first,' said Geraldine.

'I think I'm going to cry,' said Melanie.

'To cross the river, the only supplies you can use are . . .' said Geraldine. Now she positively grinned. 'Your rubbish from last week.'

'Okay, that's a weird idea,' said Friday.

'Plus, anything you can find in the forest,' added Geraldine.

All the students stared at her in appalled silence.

133

'What are you standing around waiting for? Your rubbish is waiting for you down on the riverbank. Go!'

The students took off sprinting, even the House-boaters, who secretly suspected that any attempt would be futile because they were predestined to be the losers.

'Come on,' said Friday, taking Melanie by the hand and pulling her along. 'This is going to take brains as well as brawn. We're in with a chance.'

There were four large stacks of rubbish sitting on the riverbank. The Houseboaters had the smallest stack, but it still amounted to about eight bags of garbage.

'What should we do?' asked Patel.

'Empty out the bags and see what we've got,' said Friday.

Everyone grabbed a bag and started emptying. It was mainly just food wrappers and crumpled packaging. Melanie's bag had a lot of scrunched-up paper.

'What is this?' asked Melanie.

'That's mine,' said Susan, snatching a handful of the paper away from her. But she dropped a piece near Friday's feet, and Friday could clearly see the words, 'Dear Mum and Dad, please come and rescue me', as well as some marks she could swear were tear stains.

'There's nothing terribly useful here,' said Harvey.

'What a shame none of us threw away an inflatable motorboat last week,' said Melanie.

'We can use anything from the forest,' said Patel. 'Should we start finding branches to make a canoe?'

'We could use the plastic bags as twine to tie branches together,' said Wai-Yi.

Just then, they were interrupted by yelling further up the riverbank.

'That's just stupid!' yelled Trea.

'You're stupid!' yelled Jessica.

Everyone turned to watch the Treehouse team fighting with each other. They were usually playing it too cool to raise their voices.

'This whole camp is stupid!' yelled Brandon.

'Would you all just shut up!' yelled Ian.

'At least they're not doing much better,' said Patel.

The Houseboaters watched as Ian turned away from his group and stalked down the river.

'What's he doing?' asked Melanie.

When Ian got to the riverbank he didn't stop. He dived in.

'Is he drowning himself?' asked Melanie. 'It's not like Ian to give up so easily.'

Ian resurfaced several metres into the flowing water, cutting through the current with powerful strokes.

'He's not building anything,' said Friday. 'He's just going to swim over and get the supplies!'

'But surely the current is too strong?' said Wai-Yi.

As he approached the middle of the river, the current did begin to give Ian trouble. He was being pushed further and further downstream.

'Quick,' said Friday. 'If you don't want to be hungry for the rest of the day, gather up all the garbage bags and start tying them together.'

'Why?' asked Melanie.

'We're going to make a rope,' said Friday.

The Houseboaters set to work, grabbing garbage bags and tying them end to end.

Suddenly there was a loud cheer.

They looked up to see that Ian had made it to the other side, although he was a good two hundred metres downstream thanks to the current.

'He's won,' said Patel.

'That doesn't matter,' said Friday. 'We only have to beat one of the other two teams.'

The Houseboaters looked across. The Tent team were building a raft out of sticks and tying inflated garbage bags to the underside for floatation. The Hole team were building a canoe. They had found an old log and were using tin cans to scrape the rotten wood out of the middle.

Meanwhile, Ian had run up to his team's supplies and began dragging them towards the river. It was a packaged-up cube of boxes.

'Keep working,' urged Friday.

The Houseboaters now had nearly twenty metres of rope.

On the far bank, Ian gave the supplies a big shove and they tipped over the edge into the water. His team cheered. But then the supplies sank, quickly disappearing from view.

The Treehouse team started yelling outraged abuse at him.

'What?' exclaimed Trea.

'Get our food back up!' screamed Jessica.

Ian leapt into the water, which was surprisingly deep close to the bank, and began duck-diving down to try to find the food.

'What sort of food sinks?' wondered Melanie.

'It must be canned food,' said Friday. 'There's no air in a can of food, nothing to give it buoyancy. It's just a tin can full of liquids and solids. There's no reason why it would float. It's like a box full of rocks.'

'We've got twenty-five metres of rope,' said Wai-Yi. 'I don't think there's anything else here that we could use.'

'Good,' said Friday. 'Now gather up all the big two-litre juice bottles.'

'What are you planning to use them for?' asked Susan.

'I'm going to shove them up inside my cardigan to make a buoyancy jacket,' said Friday, jamming bottles up her cardigan as she spoke. The others started helping her and she was soon looking like the Michelin man. A fuzzy brown version of the Michelin man, but the Michelin man, nonetheless.

There was a loud splash behind them. The Hole team had launched their canoe. They all cheered. Two of their team got in with makeshift paddles and they were given a push off from the bank.

'Oh dear,' said Friday.

'What?' said Melanie.

'I hope they can swim,' said Friday.

'Why?' asked Harvey.

'Watch,' said Friday.

The canoers took a couple of strokes out into the river, then they reached the full flow of the current. The water hit the side of the canoe and rolled it over, throwing both students into the river. The canoe then rolled over the top of them and went downstream.

'I don't want to fall in the river,' said Wai-Yi. 'My swimming isn't that good. I'd rather go hungry for a day.'

'Give me the rope,' said Friday. 'I've got this.' She grabbed the rope and ran up the bank.

'Where's she going?' asked Patel.

'I'd say she was running away,' said Melanie, 'but I think she'd take the thirty drink bottles out from under her cardigan if she was going to do that.'

The bank rose up several metres above the water.

'And she's having to run uphill,' said Susan. 'Poor Friday.'

Once she got to the top, they could see Friday jump up and start climbing a tree.

'She's gotten much better at tree climbing since she came to Highcrest,' observed Melanie. 'It just goes to show, even clever people can still learn something by going to school.'

Now Friday was edging her way out along a branch.

'If she dies, do you think they'll cancel the competition and let us all eat?' asked Patel hopefully.

'I should think so,' said Melanie. 'Because we'll all have to go down to the police station to fill out statements.'

Friday had climbed down and was backing away from the river.

Further up the bank, there was another splash.

The Tent team had launched their raft. It seemed a lot more stable than the canoe, and it was large.

'They'll easily be able to bring their food back in that,' said Wai-Yi.

Downstream, the Hole team had all jumped in the water and were swimming their log across the river.

'They might not be able to ride in that canoe,' said Melanie, 'but they'll be able to use it to bring the food back.'

'What's Friday doing?' asked Harvey.

They all looked up to see Friday stand still for a moment, and then run at full speed (which looked very silly with the bottles stuffed up her cardigan) towards the river.

'She's lost her mind!' worried Melanie.

Friday leapt straight off the bank four metres above the water.

'She's going to die!' screamed Susan.

But Friday had a firm grasp of the end of the rope. She swung out over the water, well past the middle of the current, before letting go and plopping down just a few metres from the far bank.

The Houseboaters erupted in screams of joy.

'I can't believe it!' cried Harvey.

'She actually knew what she was doing!' yelled Wai-Yi, grabbing Patel in a big hug.

Friday was not a good swimmer, but with thirty plastic bottles inserted in her clothes there was no way she would sink. She awkwardly paddled over to the bank.

'Quick,' said Melanie, 'let's get the rope. Then we can throw it across to help pull her back.' The Houseboat team started scrambling up the hill.

Friday made it to the nearest pile of supplies, took hold and pulled it over to the bank. She then took the empty bottles out from under her cardigan and began hooking them onto the plastic strapping around the box.

Ian was still duck-diving down into the water trying to find his sunken food. He looked over and saw what Friday was doing.

'You think you're so clever, don't you?' said Ian.

Friday had just fastened the last bottle to the package. 'I honestly hadn't given it any thought,' she said. 'Every standardised examination I have ever taken certainly supports that conclusion. But there is a theory that human intelligence can be broken up into seven different types, and I am well aware that I am a blithering idiot at emotional intelligence.'

Ian sighed and slumped on the bank, surrounded by his waterlogged supplies. 'You know, sometimes you are so pedantic that you go beyond being annoying and I can almost feel sympathy for you.'

Friday nodded. 'That's probably the oxygen starvation talking because you've had to duck-dive down under the water so many times. When you've caught your breath, I'm sure I'll start irritating you again.' She started to unbutton the fly on her jeans.

'Hey! What are you doing?' yelled Ian, leaping up and turning away so he wouldn't be subjected to any unexpected nudity.

'I've got undies on,' said Friday.

'No one wants to see your legs,' said Ian.

'I'm still wearing my cardigan and t-shirt,' said Friday. 'Get over yourself. You'd see more if I was in my swimmers.'

'But why are you taking your trousers off?' asked Ian.

'It's survival skill,' said Friday. 'I read up on them before we came away to camp. If you need to make a buoyancy vest, you just take off your trousers, tie the ankles together, get them wet, then fill them up with air and hold them around your neck.' She waded into the river. 'I'm not very good at swimming,' Friday explained as she grabbed hold of her supplies and pulled them towards her. The supplies bobbed down in the water, but with the bottles attached all around the outside, the package floated like an iceberg with ten percent above the water.

'Friday!' yelled Melanie from the far side of the river. 'Grab hold.'

Patel swung the rope around his head with his good arm. He had tied a rock to the end to give it momentum. Then he let go. It hurtled through the air.

'Watch out!' cried Ian.

'For what?' asked Friday. As she turned to glance at Ian, the rock with the rope attached hit Friday on the side of the head.

Ian winced.

Friday tottered on her feet for a moment then passed out face down in the water. Ian leapt in and grabbed her, pulling her onto her back. She floated easily in that position because of the buoyancy vest.

Ian sighed. 'The number of times I've had to rescue you.' He grabbed the one tin of sardines he'd managed to save from his own supplies, put it on top of Friday's brick, tied the rope to it, then took hold of Friday and waded out into the river.

The Houseboaters started pulling him and the package back across as they drew in the rope hand over hand.

The cool water soon made Friday regain consciousness. 'What's happening?' she asked.

'I'm saving you again,' said Ian.

'Okay,' said Friday.

'But you won the supply challenge,' said Ian. 'All I managed to retrieve was a can of sardines.'

'Never mind,' said Friday. 'The girls in your hut are keen on slimming anyway.'

Ian laughed.

The next thing Friday knew, there were five pairs of hands grabbing hold of her and the supplies as the Houseboaters waded in and helped them from the water.

'Are you all right?' asked Melanie.

'I think so,' said Friday, rubbing her head.

'It was nice of Ian to hug you as you swam back with him,' said Melanie.

'I wasn't hugging her,' said Ian. 'I was rescuing her by swimming sidestroke.'

'Ahuh,' said Melanie. 'You say "potato", I say "it looked like a nice hug".'

'The Treehouse team loses,' announced Geraldine, glaring scornfully at her favourite team.

The Tent team and the Hole team were working together to bring back the one remaining block of supplies in the canoe. The third block of supplies was still at the bottom of the river, no doubt well on its way downstream towards the ocean.

'The Tent and Hole people can share their supplies,' said Geraldine. 'The Treehouse team will spend a whole day going without.'

'It's all your fault, Wainscott,' said Jessica bitterly.

'We should throw him out for fraternising with the enemy,' said Mirabella.

'Hang about,' said Drake. 'Wainscott is our best athlete. You don't want to cut your nose off to spite your face.'

Mirabella gasped in horror. 'Who told you I've had plastic surgery?!'

'What?' asked Drake, terrified of the reaction he'd caused. 'It's just an expression. Cut your nose off to . . .'

'How dare you!' yelled Mirabella. She launched herself at Drake trying to slap him, but he dived into the river to get away. 'Come back here, you coward!'

'Stop!' called Friday. 'There's no need to be angry with Drake or Wainscott, I mean, Ian.'

'They're on a first-name basis,' said Melanie.

'You won't go hungry,' said Friday. 'We'll share our supplies with you.'

'We will?' asked Patel.

'But they're always mean to us,' protested Wai-Yi.

'I know,' said Friday. 'But if I'd drowned on the other bank, we wouldn't be getting anything to eat either. We wouldn't have got the supplies without Ian's help.'

'That sounds fair enough,' said Harvey.

'There are only six of us,' said Melanie, 'so there would be extra to share.'

'It's a deal, then,' said Friday.

'Thank you,' said Ian.

'But don't think this means that we like you, Barnes,' said Trea.

'I would be horrified if you did,' said Friday.

Chapter 13

▰▰▰▰▰▰▰▰▰▰▰▰▰▰▰▰▰

Petty Thief

'Barnes, I need your help.'

Friday looked up from the potato she was peeling. She was a scruffy person at the best of times, but having just peeled her 183rd potato since her pre-dawn star Friday was even more dishevelled and dirt-smeared than usual. So she provided stark contrast to Jessica Dawes, the lean, athletic strawberry-blonde standing before her. Jessica was wearing jeans and a t-shirt the same as Friday, but unlike Friday her clothes were immaculate.

'Did you bring an iron?' asked Friday.

'What?' asked Jessica.

'Your clothes are perfect,' said Friday, 'no creases or crumples. Did you bring an iron with you to camp?'

'Of course not,' said Jessica. 'We're meant to be roughing it here.'

'So how are your clothes so beautiful?' asked Friday.

'It all comes down to how you fold them when you pack,' explained Jessica. 'Our maid always uses tissue paper between the clothes so that they don't get crumpled.'

'I see,' said Friday. She nodded and went back to peeling potatoes.

'I need your help,' continued Jessica.

'I have another 117 potatoes to peel before breakfast,' said Friday. 'If you want to tell me your problem, you'll have to do it while I peel. Better yet, you could pick up a peeler and help.'

Jessica snorted a laugh. 'I can't do that. If anyone from my hut sees me talking to you, let alone helping you, I'd never hear the end of it. They'd probably make me sleep on the verandah. And I toss and turn, so I might fall over the side of the Treehouse.'

'And that would be a terrible shame,' said Friday. (She was getting better at sarcasm. This was precisely the sort of important social skill that Friday went to high school to learn.)

'Someone has been stealing my breakfast cereal,' whispered Jessica.

Friday looked up from her potato. She was clearly missing something. The camp for all its faults – and there were a great many – did provide a full hot breakfast for the campers every morning. You could even go back and get seconds, or thirds if you were particularly hungry and didn't mind watery scrambled eggs or fatty bacon.

'So why don't you help yourself to more?' Friday asked.

Jessica was puzzled for a second then she caught on. 'Oh no, it's not the breakfast cereal they provide, that horrible stuff full of sulphites, sugar and carbohydrates.'

'Carbohydrates are sugars,' said Friday.

'They're all unhealthy,' said Jessica.

'You'd die if you didn't eat any sugar,' said Friday. 'There's fructose in fruit, lactose in milk, sucrose in sugar cane and galactose in sugar beets. You can't get away from sugar.'

'My dietician says I need to if I'm going to achieve one per cent body fat,' said Jessica.

'Why on earth would you want to achieve one per cent body fat?' asked Friday.

'So I can make Trea Babcock die with envy,' said Jessica.

'All right,' said Friday, 'let's set your frightening lack of understanding of the chemistry of food aside, and move on with the problem at hand. I take it you have a stash of breakfast cereal you brought from home and someone is stealing that?'

'Yes, my breakfast cereal is paleo, gluten-free, probiotic and high in protein,' said Jessica.

'So is a slice of bacon,' said Friday.

'But bacon is high in fat,' said Jessica.

'You need fat in your diet for fingernails, hair and essential minerals,' said Friday.

'If I'm bald, I can wear a wig,' said Jessica. 'If I'm fat, there's nothing I can do about that.'

Friday sighed. She didn't know why she bothered using facts and reasoned argument on girls like Jessica.

'So someone has been taking your breakfast cereal,' said Friday.

'Yes, every morning when I wake up, the jar has been pulled out from under my bed, the lid has been taken off and some cereal is missing,' said Jessica. 'You're supposed to be a detective. I want you to find out who's been stealing it.'

'What's in it for me?' asked Friday.

'What?' asked Jessica.

'How are you going to pay me?' asked Friday.

'This is a camp,' said Jessica. 'We're meant to be roughing it. We were specifically told not to bring money.'

'You brought paleo, gluten-free, probiotic, high-protein breakfast cereal, but you didn't bring a credit card?' said Friday.

'You take credit cards?' asked Jessica.

'As a matter of fact, I do,' said Friday. 'We're allowed to send letters. I'll send your card number and expiry to my uncle, and he can deduct the money from your account.'

'Fine,' said Jessica.

Friday grabbed her backpack and went with Jessica back to her hut. Technically, Friday didn't really go 'with' Jessica, because Jessica insisted that Friday walk parallel to her but twenty metres away through the forest so no one would see them walking together.

'This is ridiculous,' said Friday. 'Everyone is at breakfast. No one will see us.'

'I'm not prepared to take that risk,' said Jessica.

Friday had added a 25 per cent 'being forced to walk through the forest' levy to the original fee she had negotiated, so she wasn't too fussed about Jessica's ludicrous over-precaution.

When Friday arrived at the clearing, she had to admit she was impressed. She had not seen the Treehouse close up before, and it was an amazing building. It had been built into the branches of two adjacent oak trees. There was a circular room around the trunk of each tree with a large covered communal room suspended between the two, and wide verandahs spreading out from the structure on all sides.

'Okay, that is worth doing twenty push-ups for,' conceded Friday.

'Huh?' asked Jessica.

'Never mind,' said Friday. 'Do you want to show me the scene of the crime?'

'Okay,' said Jessica, 'but if anybody sees you with me, I'm going to tell them that you forced me to let you inside by blackmailing me.'

'Blackmailing you for what?' asked Friday.

'I don't know,' said Jessica, 'I'll make something up. I'll say you're holding my poodle to ransom.'

'I would never do that,' said Friday. 'I don't like dogs.'

'Neither do I,' said Jessica, 'which is why I don't have one. But no one needs to know that. This way . . .'

Jessica led Friday over to the spiral staircase that wrapped around the trunk of the oak tree.

'The girls' dorm is in this tree,' explained Jessica. 'The boys are in the other.'

When Friday entered the dorm room she was shocked. It was immaculate. She had expected that the pampered girls, when forced to fend for themselves, would be struggling, but the room was spotless. The beds were all perfectly made with neat, crisp hospital corners. There was even a vase of wildflowers on a table in the middle of the room.

'Wow,' said Friday. 'I hadn't expected you to be so tidy.'

'Oh, we're not,' said Jessica. 'Amelie snuck in her maid.'

'Huh?' said Friday. 'Are you saying one of the girls smuggled in a human being in her luggage?'

'Gosh, no,' said Jessica. 'We had to carry our own bags. There's no way Amelie could have carried Gretchen up here. No, her father dropped the maid off at the nearest fire trail. She hiked in and is secretly camping three kilometres away in the woods. She comes in every morning before dawn to do the cleaning.'

'So which is your bed?' asked Friday.

'Over here,' said Jessica, walking over to the bed nearest to the window. She reached underneath and pulled out a large plastic jar, which was now only a third full of breakfast cereal.

'I see,' said Friday, taking the jar from Jessica and inspecting it closely. There were some scratch marks about the jar and lid, but only the normal type you would expect from kitchen Tupperware that had regular use. Friday left the jar on the bed and looked around.

'Your maid has done a thorough job of destroying all the evidence,' said Friday. 'There are no footprints, no traces of residue that may have been brought in on the perpetrator's feet, no litter left behind.'

'Excuse me if we in the Treehouse like to maintain standards,' said Jessica.

'You mean, you like to pay others to maintain your standards for you,' said Friday.

'Same thing,' said Jessica.

Friday went over and looked out the window. There wasn't much to see, just the big tree branches stretching out above and below the Treehouse.

'The problem with cleaning up a crime scene is now I have no clues,' said Friday. 'Footprints can tell me the size of a perpetrator's feet, and the length of their gait from which I can extrapolate their height. Residue from their shoes can tell me where they've been. And accidentally dropped litter can tell me what they've been up to. I have none of that here.'

Jessica sighed. 'I'm not really interested in what you can't do. I want to know what you *can* do.'

'I could cross-examine all your roommates,' said Friday.

Jessica scoffed at the thought. 'Not going to happen. I don't want people to see me with you, and I certainly don't want them to know I've spoken to you.'

'All right,' said Friday. 'Then I suppose all I can do is fingerprint the jar.'

'You can do that?' asked Jessica.

'Sure. All I need is some powder, sticky tape, a brush and some black card,' said Friday. 'Do you have those things here?'

'Duh,' said Jessica. 'What do you think this is? A preschool? I didn't bring craft supplies.'

'You probably have some of them,' said Friday. 'We just need to think laterally. Did you bring any make-up with you?'

'Of course,' said Jessica. 'My mother never lets me leave the house without all the essential supplies.'

'So does that include blush?' asked Friday.

'Yes,' said Jessica.

'May I borrow it?' asked Friday.

'Why? You never wear make-up,' said Jessica.

'Just lend it to me and I'll show you,' said Friday.

Jessica went to her make-up bag, rifled through and found a blush compact.

'Perfect,' said Friday. 'Now we just need to find the fingerprints on the jar.'

Friday very carefully took hold of the jar by the rim of the base, then with her other hand began liberally shaking powder all over the container.

'Hey!' exclaimed Jessica. 'That's from Paris. It costs $100 a jar.'

'Do you want me to take these fingerprints or not?' asked Friday.

'Fine,' sulked Jessica.

Friday shook the loose powder off the jar, then peered closely at the surface. 'There's something here, hand me the brush,' she said.

Jessica held onto the brush petulantly. 'Why, what are you going to do with it?'

'I'm going to brush the powder,' said Friday. 'Isn't that what it's for?'

Jessica reluctantly handed over the soft make-up brush, and Friday carefully wiped the excess powder away.

'Aha!' said Friday. 'I've got one.'

Friday opened her bag and took out her sticky tape. She gently laid the sticky tape across the fingerprint, then lifted it up.

'Now I just need something black or at least dark to stick it to,' said Friday. 'Do you have a book with a dark cover?'

'Yeah, right,' said Jessica. 'Like any of us brought books. We're not nerds.'

'Okay,' said Friday, looking about the room for inspiration. 'Did any of you sneak in a smartphone?'

'Of course not,' said Jessica. 'That's against the rules.'

'Please,' said Friday, rolling her eyes, 'you can't expect me to believe that.'

'Okay,' said Jessica, going over to her bed and lifting up the mattress.

The latest, fanciest smartphone was lying underneath. It had a hot-pink diamanté case, but when Friday took the case off, the phone itself was black.

'Perfect,' said Friday. She lay the sticky tape across the black case and suddenly the fingerprint was visible. It wasn't a fingerprint. It was a whole handprint.

'Eww!' said Jessica. 'What's wrong with them? Their fingerprints are tiny. Are you saying a midget stole my breakfast cereal?'

'No, I would never say that, because it would be rude and insensitive to small people,' said Friday. 'These aren't human fingerprints. They are the fingerprints of a possum.'

'Huh?' said Jessica.

'You know, "huh" is never an adequate word to express yourself,' said Friday. 'Certainly not in the wide number of contexts in which you insist on using it.'

'How can a possum come in here and open a jar?' asked Jessica.

'Well, if I were the possum,' said Friday, 'I would be wondering why ten humans were living in my tree. This is his natural habitat.'

'But surely he can't open a jar?' said Jessica.

'Why not?' said Friday. 'Possums don't have opposable thumbs, but they have very manipulative digits. They can perform extraordinary acts of dexterity when climbing from tree to tree, so why not open a jar as well? If you want further proof, ask Gretchen about the droppings.'

'What droppings?' asked Jessica.

'After eating such a healthy, paleo, gluten-free, probiotic, high-protein meal every night,' said Friday, 'I'm 100 per cent certain that the possum would have pooed here somewhere. Gretchen will know. There's no doubt about it. The criminal mastermind behind this theft is a common possum.'

Just then, the door swung open.

'What's she doing here?' demanded Trea. She and the other Treehouse girls had returned from breakfast.

'She broke in!' lied Jessica. 'She's been stealing my breakfast cereal.' She leapt back and pointed at

Friday, literally putting as much distance between herself and the most reviled girl in year 7.

'Pathetic,' said Mirabella. 'Did you want to see how the other half live?'

'*Quarter*,' corrected Friday. 'A quarter of the year lives in this Treehouse. So if I were intrigued by your lifestyle, it would be because I wanted to see how the other *quarter* lives.'

'Whatever,' said Trea. 'Just get out.'

'Fine,' said Friday, heading for the door. 'But, Jessica, unless you want a raging case of possum flu, I wouldn't eat the rest of that breakfast cereal you've been hiding from your roommates.'

As Friday walked away, she could practically feel the glares of hatred boring into her back.

Chapter 14

▰▰▰▰▰▰▰▰▰▰▰▰▰▰▰▰

Colour War

'Good morning, maggots,' yelled Geraldine. She was standing at the front of the dining room making a breakfast-time announcement.

'What is her obsession with larval-stage house-flies?' asked Friday.

'I think she just enjoys the way the word rolls off the tongue,' said Melanie.

'You've been here at camp for three weeks, so now it's time to test how much you've learned,' announced Geraldine.

'Please let it be a multiple-choice exam paper, please let it be a multiple-choice exam paper ...' muttered Patel under his breath as he crossed all his fingers and toes.

'We are going to have a Colour War!' declared Geraldine.

The Treehouse and Tent teams cheered. The Hole team glowered and the Houseboaters openly groaned.

'Survival is all about survival of the fittest ...' continued Geraldine.

'That's just not true,' muttered Friday.

'Did you have something to say, Barnes?' yelled Geraldine.

Friday tried to disappear into the floor using nothing but the power of her mind, but her attempts at telekinesis were in vain.

'On your feet when I'm talking to you!' bellowed Geraldine.

Friday stood up, bracing herself for whatever verbal or even physical assault was coming.

'Did you have something to say?' demanded Geraldine.

'Just that survival isn't always about survival of the fittest,' said Friday.

'I thought you were a smartypants,' said Geraldine. 'Haven't you ever heard of a scientist called Charles Darwin?' The whole dining hall full of kids sniggered. Even the dopier Highcrest Academy students had heard of Darwin and his theory of evolution.

'Yes, but sometimes group work and self-sacrifice is more important for survival,' said Friday. 'Ants, bees, baboons and elephants all work as communities to ensure their survival.'

'Well, I'm sure if your team of losers are confronted by a herd of elephants during the Colour War, they will find that fact very comforting,' said Geraldine.

Again everyone chuckled. People instinctively enjoyed watching someone else being bullied. Largely because it's not them.

Friday sat down. 'The benchmark for humour is so much lower for bullies,' she mumbled.

'What was that?' snapped Geraldine.

'I'm glad I packed my woollies,' said Friday.

'Woolly what?' asked Geraldine.

'Cardigans,' said Friday. 'To survive. It's so important to stay warm.'

Geraldine evidently decided she wasn't winning

this conversation so she turned back to the rest of the group, ignoring Friday.

'Today you will all face several tests,' said Geraldine. 'At the end of the competition, the team with the highest score wins.'

'What do we win?' called out Ian.

Geraldine smiled at him. He was her favourite. She liked handsome boys. Especially handsome athletic boys who cheated in games. They reminded Geraldine of her young self.

'You win first choice of destination on the survival challenge,' said Geraldine.

'The what?' muttered Mirabella.

'We have a surprise for you,' announced Geraldine. 'The last three days of camp will be a survival challenge. You will hike out into the bush for three days with only minimal provisions so you can put into practice all the survival skills you've learned.'

'But all we've learned is how to dig a latrine,' said Patel.

'That's not true,' said Melanie. 'Friday can peel a potato.'

'If we dig up any potatoes while we're digging a latrine, that will be helpful,' said Harvey.

'Trust me, you want to pick where you're going for the wilderness challenge,' said Geraldine. 'Some of the options are deeply unpleasant.' She smirked at the Houseboat table as she said this.

Chapter 15

First Round

Ten minutes later, all the students were gathered down by the riverbank.

'The first challenge is lighting a fire,' announced Geraldine. 'Do any of you have matches or a lighter on you?'

The students shook their heads.

Friday held her hand up. 'I've got both.'

'Hand them over,' said Geraldine.

Sebastian stepped forward and took the lighter and matches from her. Friday noticed he had dark bags under his eyes. He looked like he hadn't had any sleep. Perhaps being a camp counsellor was way more stressful than it seemed.

'You must light a fire using only things you find in nature or what you have on you right now,' continued Geraldine. 'The team that finishes first will get three points, the team that comes second will get two points, the third one point, and the team that comes last –' Geraldine grinned at the Houseboaters '– will get zero. Does everybody understand?'

'Actually, could you explain the bit about . . .' began Patel.

'Good, then on your marks, get set, GO!'

Students started running off in the bush in every direction.

The Houseboaters instinctively turned to Friday.

'What should we do?' asked Wai-Yi.

'Does anybody have a battery?' asked Friday.

The whole group shook their heads.

Friday glanced about. 'This area does not have the right geology for finding a sedimentary crypto-crystalline form of mineral quartz, so we've got no chance of finding naturally occurring flint. And it's been drizzling for the last few days, but there haven't been any lightning strikes so there is no hope of finding a smouldering log.' Friday looked up at the sky, just as the sun came out from behind a bank of clouds. She turned to her team of nerds and misfits, and smiled. 'We can do this.'

'We can?' asked Melanie. 'Because you know we could always give up now and conserve our energy for the next challenge.'

'No, we've got this,' said Friday. 'Patel, take your shirt off!'

'What?' cried Patel, clutching his chest protectively.

'We need tinder,' said Friday. 'Tiny strands of highly flammable material. Normally in the wild you'd use bark or tree moss.'

'That's what the other teams are using,' said Wai-Yi as she looked about.

'But it's been drizzling for days,' said Friday. 'That will all be damp. Whereas Patel's shirt is entirely dry and is made of cotton, so it is highly flammable. We just need to tear it to shreds.'

Wai-Yi and Susan grabbed Patel and started yanking off his shirt.

'But that's my favourite shirt!' protested Patel.

'It's a plain grey t-shirt,' said Susan. 'We'll buy you a new one when this is all over.'

'I'll get cold,' argued Patel.

'Don't worry,' said Friday. 'Soon you'll be able to warm yourself by our fire.'

Friday handed Wai-Yi her penknife and the shirt was soon transformed into tiny strips of rags.

'Now, who here has the thickest lens in their glasses?' asked Friday.

Susan, Wai-Yi, Harvey and Patel were all wearing glasses.

'My right eye is a 3 and my left eye a 2.25,' volunteered Wai-Yi.

'I'm just a 2 in each eye,' said Susan.

'I'm a 3 in my left eye and an 8 in my right,' confessed Harvey.

'Wow!' said Patel.

'Doesn't that make you legally blind?' asked Melanie.

'No, technically I would have to be 6/60 vision or be worse in my right eye as well,' said Harvey.

'We're going to use the lens from your glasses to magnify the sun,' said Friday.

'We've got a spark!' cried Ian.

The Houseboaters looked over to see the Treehouse team standing around as Ian athletically worked a hand drill made from sticks.

'Snap out of it, Friday!' said Melanie. 'You haven't got time to ogle Ian now.'

'I wasn't ogling,' said Friday.

'Of course not,' said Melanie. 'I'm sure you were forensically observing his rippling muscles purely for scientific reasons.'

Friday took Harvey's glasses and held them between the sun and the tinder. Immediately a concentrated patch of light was focused in on the cloth.

'You'd better go and find some twigs,' said Friday. 'Once we get a flame, we'll need to make it into a fire.'

'But everything is wet,' said Melanie.

'Look underneath fallen logs and search for mushrooms,' said Friday.

'We don't have time to cook,' argued Melanie.

'Mushrooms can be flammable,' explained Friday.

'We've done it!'

Friday looked up to see that the Hole team had got their fire going now. Only the Tent team was still working and they seemed to be making good progress.

'Can I smell smoke?' asked Harvey. He hadn't gone off into the forest to search for twigs because without his glasses he was as blind as a bat.

Friday looked down at her tinder. 'It's starting to smoke!' she exclaimed.

'Aren't you meant to blow on it?' asked Harvey.

'Of course, increase oxygen supply,' said Friday. 'Good thinking.' She bent over and gently blew on the smouldering cloth.

Soon she had a flame. 'I've got it!' exclaimed Friday.

'I can't believe it worked,' said Harvey.

'Now we just need kindling,' said Friday.

'Here you go,' said Susan.

Friday looked up just as Susan dumped her kindling onto the newly lit flame. The fire was immediately quashed.

'That's not fungus,' said Friday. 'That's moss.'

'What's the difference?' asked Susan.

'They are an entirely different genus for a start,' said Friday. 'But the principal practical difference in this situation is one is wet and one is dry. You picked the wet one.'

'Whoops,' said Susan.

'We've got fire!' yelled Tabitha from the Tent team.

The Houseboaters groaned.

'That's zero points to your team, Barnes,' said Geraldine gleefully.

'Was that my fault?' asked Susan.

'Only completely,' said Melanie, giving Susan's shoulder a comforting pat.

'Never mind,' said Patel. 'Maybe we'll do better in the next challenge.'

Friday smiled at him. The boy was clearly delusional but she had to admire his optimism.

Chapter 16

Melanie's Secret

The next challenge was to take place on the field, although it wasn't really much of a field. Clearly no one had ever watered it. It was more of a dirt patch held together by grass tufts, but it was about the same size as a football field so energetic students who didn't mind getting filthy were able to play ball sports there.

As the students milled at the far end of the field waiting for Geraldine and the other counsellors, they muttered nervously amongst themselves.

'What do you think she'll have us doing now?' asked Patel.

'If she was sensible, she'd have us reseeding the grass and aerating the soil,' said Friday. 'It would be a physical challenge and it would improve the lawn no end.'

'Well, she's not going to do that, then,' said Melanie.

'Right, maggots,' said Geraldine. 'This should be fun.' She was riding in the back of an old red ute, which pulled up alongside the group of students. Geraldine awkwardly hopped out. It's hard enough for anybody to jump athletically out of the back of a ute, let alone an overweight middle-aged woman with a prosthetic leg. So she stumbled a bit. Luckily Ian was nearby to step forward and steady her.

'Are you all right?' asked Ian.

'Yes, yes,' said Geraldine. 'Stupid leg. Doesn't have enough give in it. Can't even use it for firewood, because they don't make the things out of wood anymore.'

The ute drove away towards the other end of the field.

'So what's the next challenge?' asked Friday, eyeing the ute with suspicion.

'It's a good one,' said Geraldine. 'In the wild you need to be able to hunt.'

Patel groaned. 'She's going to make us hunt wild pigs with our bare hands, I just know it!'

'We're not allowed to make you do real hunting anymore,' said Geraldine, 'because of those animal rights softies, but we can make you shoot arrows at timber cut-outs.'

Geraldine pointed to the far end of the field where the counsellors were unloading four coloured cut-outs. 'The first team to hit their target five times wins.'

'But they're three hundred metres away,' protested Ian.

'An accomplished marksman can hit a target twice that distance,' said Geraldine.

'But we're not accomplished marksmen,' said Ian.

'Not yet,' said Geraldine. 'But you will be, if you're here all day trying.'

'Which team gets which target?' asked Friday. The cut-outs were being set up now and she'd noticed that the four shapes were not the same.

'The Treehouse gets the blue bear,' began Geraldine, 'the Tent gets the red deer, the Hole gets the yellow buffalo and the Houseboat gets the brown frog.'

The other teams laughed as they saw this final shape being put up.

'But it's much smaller than the other three!' protested Friday. 'It must be a third of the surface area of the buffalo or the bear.'

'Tough,' said Geraldine.

'And it's a lot harder to see a brown frog on a dirt field than it is to see the other colours,' said Friday.

'Boohoo,' continued Geraldine sarcastically.

'Friday,' whispered Melanie, tugging on her friend's arm.

'Not now,' said Friday. 'This isn't fair . . .'

'Friday, listen to me. Let it go!' said Melanie. She was quite insistent now.

This caught Friday's attention. Her best friend rarely became animated about anything. 'What is it?' she asked.

Melanie drew Friday aside. 'I don't want you to think less of me for what I am about to reveal to you.'

'Why?' asked Friday with growing dread. 'You're not going to tell me you are ethically opposed to harming cut-outs, are you?'

'Goodness, no,' said Melanie. 'I've never liked cut-outs, not since the time I spent five minutes talking to Harrison Ford at a shopping centre before I realised it was a two-dimensional cardboard representation of Han Solo.'

'So?' said Friday.

'So what?' asked Melanie.

'What is the shocking thing you're going to reveal about yourself?' asked Friday.

Melanie leaned in and whispered, 'We're going to win this challenge.'

'What?' asked Friday.

Melanie nodded.

'How?' asked Friday.

Melanie leaned in and whispered very quietly, 'I'm extremely good at archery.'

'No way,' said Friday.

Melanie shrugged. 'It's true.'

'How did that happen?' asked Friday.

'As you know,' said Melanie, 'Mummy and Daddy are very rich. And when we were little, they were forever having us coached at things. You know, the boys were coached in rugby and tennis and swimming and cricket . . .'

'I get the picture,' said Friday.

'So one year, Jub took an interest in archery and the coach was teaching him on the back lawn,' explained Melanie. 'He was a very nice coach, extremely patient. And short. I like short people. They're less confusing, I find . . .'

'And he encouraged you to try archery?' prompted Friday, trying to get her friend back on topic.

'Yes,' said Melanie. 'And the thing was, right away I was very good.'

'Really?' said Friday.

'And when I practised I got seriously very good,' said Melanie.

'But you have no aptitude for any other physical endeavour,' said Friday.

'Apparently it's because I'm so calm,' said Melanie. 'Most people naturally have tremors in their hands or their bodies, which makes it hard to hold the bow still, but I am so very good at being relaxed I can stay completely still.'

'I believe you,' said Friday. 'I've seen you do it.'

'If I'm really super-duper still, I can sense my own heartbeat and time my shot so that it falls between beats,' said Melanie.

'No way,' said Friday.

'That's what all the best archers do,' explained Melanie.

'Just how good were you?' asked Friday.

'There was no chance I could compete at the Olympics –' said Melanie.

'Of course not,' said Friday.

'– but only because I was too young,' said Melanie. 'You have to be sixteen to be included in the archery team now.'

'Wow,' said Friday.

'Yes, now you know my dark secret,' said Melanie.

'I can't believe you didn't mention it before,' said Friday.

'Archery is not a subject that often comes up,' said Melanie, 'so I can go months at a time without remembering myself.'

And so Melanie made short work of the archery. The chosen archers for each of the other teams had only fired off a couple of misjudged practice shots in the time it took Melanie to skewer the brown frog five times between the eyes.

'How did you do that?' asked Ian, coming over to shake her hand.

'It's easy, really,' said Melanie. 'You just point the pointy thing at the target and let it go.'

'Come on, it's not that simple,' said Friday.

'Well, you do have to allow for wind speed and the parabolic angle of ascent over this sort of distance,' admitted Melanie. 'But parabolas are easy, the maths teachers drone on about them all the time. I'm surprised the rest of you haven't picked it up.'

'I don't think I've ever enjoyed being beaten at anything so much,' said Ian, shaking his head in wonder.

While the Houseboaters congratulated Melanie, Friday couldn't help overhearing a very quiet argument taking place behind her. She turned to see who it was, expecting it to be the sulky Treehouse team again. But it wasn't. It was two of the counsellors, having an argument but trying to keep their voices down at the same time.

'*You* check on them!' whispered Sebastian.

'She'll notice if I leave,' whispered Nadia.

'They need water,' said Sebastian. 'We can't lose our investment. Not when we're so close.'

'All right,' said Nadia.

'Don't forget the ghost,' said Sebastian.

Nadia nodded.

As the students were shepherded on to the next challenge, Nadia slipped away in the other direction, towards the river.

'What was that all about?' wondered Friday.

'What?' said Melanie. 'Were Nadia and Sebastian fighting again?'

'You've seen them doing it before?' asked Friday.

'My mattress is by the window,' said Melanie. 'I woke up one night last week, and heard them having a conversation on the riverbank.'

'What were they talking about?' asked Friday.

'Cheese,' said Melanie.

'What?' said Friday. 'You must have misheard. Why would they be talking about cheese in the middle of the night?'

'Because it's delicious,' suggested Melanie.

The rest of the Colour War progressed in much the same way. The Houseboat team did abysmally at anything involving physical exertion. So they came last in rowing, rock skipping and tree climbing. But they did slightly better at anything where thinking helped. So they did okay at knot tying, compass reading and fungus identifying (Larissa Hatton had to be rushed to hospital after she had misidentified a mushroom and eaten it as a snack). Surprisingly, the Houseboat team did well at woodchopping because they'd had so much practice.

And so it all came down to the last event. The Treehouse team had 23 points; the Tent, 22; the Hole, 22; and the Houseboat, 21.

'Theoretically we could win,' said Friday.

'But only if the other teams lose in the exact right order,' added Patel.

'Yes, but it is mathematically possible, even if highly improbable,' said Friday.

'The last event is a simple one,' announced Geraldine. 'It is a footrace.'

The Houseboat team groaned. They all knew they were terrible at running.

'But there's a twist,' added Geraldine.

'Are you going to release a bear?' asked Melanie.

'What?' asked Geraldine.

'I just thought people would probably run faster if you released a bear behind them,' explained Melanie.

'Be quiet if you haven't got anything sensible to say!' said Geraldine, shaking her head. 'It will be a normal race with just humans, except that it will be a piggyback race.'

'But pigs aren't humans,' said Melanie. 'They aren't, are they?' she asked Friday.

Friday shook her head.

'One person from each team will carry another person around the course,' said Geraldine.

Ian put up his hand. 'Do we have to carry someone from our own team?'

Geraldine thought about it for a moment. 'I don't see why. You can carry whoever you like.'

'Then I'm carrying Friday,' declared Ian.

'No, you're not!' said Friday.

'You have to. Geraldine said so,' said Ian.

'No, she didn't,' said Friday.

'I'm making it a rule right now. If you're picked, then you have to be carried,' said Geraldine.

'I want to carry Wai-Yi!' yelled Harrison from the Hole team.

'Hey!' protested Wai-Yi.

'Hang about,' argued Patel, 'you can't pick all the people from our team. There will be no one left for me to carry!'

'You've got all the small, weedy people in your team,' said Drake. 'I'll carry Susan.'

'What?!' exclaimed Susan.

'I'm thinner than her,' argued Trea Babcock.

'Yeah, but you look emotionally harder to carry,' said Drake. (This was a polite way of saying that Trea was not very nice.)

'I don't want to be carried by Drake!' exclaimed Susan. 'It would be awful.'

'Shush,' said Melanie, giving Susan a nudge. 'He just paid you a lovely compliment.'

'He did?' asked Susan.

'Oh yes, when a boy thinks about carrying you around, that shows his mind is working in the right direction,' said Melanie.

'Who's going to do the carrying for our team?' asked Patel. 'Please don't say it will be me.'

'I'll do it,' said Harvey.

'But you can barely see,' said Melanie. 'And I mean that in the nicest possible way.'

'That's okay,' said Harvey. 'Whoever I'm carrying can steer me in the right direction.'

'So who do you want to carry?' asked Friday.

'No offence, Melanie,' said Harvey, 'but I think Patel may weigh a little less than you.'

'Oh, I don't mind,' said Melanie. 'I'd carry Patel too if I had the choice, but in my case that would mainly be because it's impossible to carry yourself.'

At last, Ian, Harvey, Drake and Harrison lined up with Friday, Patel, Susan and Wai-Yi.

'This is so embarrassing,' said Patel.

'We embarrass ourselves dozens of times each day,' said Harvey. 'This is just going to be one blip on the list of embarrassing things people remember you for.'

'Thanks for the motivational pep talk,' said Patel.

'Why do you need a pep talk? You're not doing anything,' said Harvey.

'I could steer you into the river if you're going to keep being depressing,' said Patel.

'All right,' said Harvey. 'Go, team! Does that make you feel better?'

'Marginally,' said Patel.

'Get up, then,' said Ian, turning around and crouching in front of Friday.

'Why didn't you pick somebody else?' asked Friday.

'Because you're short and skinny,' said Ian. 'Besides I'm used to carrying you, the number of times I've had to rescue you from things.'

'Get up there, Barnes!' yelled Geraldine. 'We haven't got time to dilly-dally around while you fuss about.'

Friday stepped forward, wrapped her arms around Ian's neck and jumped up onto his back. Melanie burst into a round of applause. Everyone stared at her.

'Sorry, I've just been waiting for something like this for so long now,' said Melanie, dabbing a tear away from the corner of her eye.

'Racers ready,' said Geraldine, holding what looked alarmingly like a real gun above her head. 'On your marks, get set . . .'

BANG!

The pistol fired and the four boys set off running. It was a lot jigglier than Friday would have cared for. Ian was a smooth runner, but not when he was carrying an awkward weight and across uneven ground.

They were halfway down the course. Ian had just started to build up speed when something ran into the back of him. Friday felt him fall out from underneath her, but she had so much forward momentum she flew straight over his head, flipping over and landing hard on her back. The wind was totally knocked out of her. Friday closed her eyes as she struggled to catch her breath. She could hear yelling and screaming. Were people screaming because they'd been knocked over too?

Friday opened her eyes. People were running. And away from her. They were running towards the finish line. Friday looked about. Ian was picking himself up from the ground just a few metres away. Drake and Susan were sprawled across the ground as well.

'What's happening?' asked Friday.

'We just lost the race,' said Ian.

'Then who won?' asked Friday.

In the distance suddenly Patel was hoisted up on the shoulders of the crowd, and then more awkwardly, Harvey was hoisted up too.

'We won!' exclaimed Friday. 'I can't believe it. Our team won!'

Chapter 17

The Triumphant Return

The Houseboaters were in a jubilant mood as they made their way up the riverbank towards their home.

'It's the first time I've ever done anything athletic,' marvelled Harvey.

'All you needed was a seeing-eye Patel,' said Melanie.

'My dad is going to be so proud,' said Harvey. 'He wanted me to become a rugby player, just like him.

He was so disappointed when I inherited his thighs but my mother's eyesight.'

It was beginning to get dark. The team were going back to wash up before dinner. Winning the Colour War had been a messy business. Apart from getting covered in dust and dirt and sweat, they had a lot of scratches and scrapes that needed first aid. They wanted to get inside where it was light so they could have a proper look at what they had done to themselves.

'Hey Wai-Yi, look over there in the river,' said Susan. 'Isn't that your pillow?'

Wai-Yi had brought a hypoallergenic pillow from home. It was distinctive because it had a pillowcase with pink unicorns.

The group squinted and peered out across the river. There was definitely something pink and unicorny floating down the middle.

'Not my pillow!' cried Wai-Yi. 'How did that get there?'

'And is that Susan's humidifier?' asked Melanie.

There was a white and blue electrical appliance bobbing about in the water. Now they looked closely there were lots of things floating in the river.

'Hurry up,' urged Friday. 'We've got to get back to find out what happened.'

They started running up the bank. It was only a few hundred metres, so they soon stumbled into the clearing where the Houseboat was moored. Except the Houseboat wasn't there.

'Are we in the right spot?' asked Harvey.

'Yes,' said Friday. 'Look, there's the jetty it's usually moored to.'

'And there's the tree I threw up on after too many tacos on Taco Tuesday,' said Patel. 'I'd recognise it anywhere.'

Friday walked out onto the jetty. There was something lying on the decking. 'It's an axe,' she said, bending over to pick it up.

'Someone was chopping firewood on the jetty?' asked Melanie.

Friday leaned over to the mooring rope. It had been cut. It was already starting to fray where a mess had been made of severing it.

'This axe was used to cut the mooring ropes,' said Friday. 'But the ropes are thick and it took them a few swings to get through.'

'Who would do something like that?' asked Susan.

'Someone who doesn't like us,' said Wai-Yi.

'That could be anybody,' said Patel.

'But where has the Houseboat gone?' asked Melanie.

'There's only one way it could go,' said Friday. 'Downstream.'

They looked in the direction the water was flowing. It was getting hard to see in the twilight. Even so, there was definitely no sign of a house on the river.

'Come on,' said Friday. 'We need to look for it, or we're not going to have anywhere to sleep tonight.'

'But what about the ghost?' said Susan. 'We're not meant to wander about at night.'

'It's not dark yet,' said Friday.

The team took off jogging down the river.

'Surely we can't catch up with the Houseboat on foot,' said Patel.

'It could be floating in the ocean by now,' said Harvey.

'I doubt it,' said Friday. 'We can't be far behind, because we saw all those things that must have fallen off. And it won't get far. It's too big. It will get snagged on something.'

'Didn't Sebastian say there was a waterfall downstream?' said Melanie.

Everyone turned and looked at Melanie.

'Run faster,' urged Friday.

They started sprinting down the bank.

'What's that noise?' asked Susan.

There was a rumbling sound up ahead.

'It sounds like a big engine,' said Wai-Yi.

'No,' said Friday. 'That's the sound of a waterfall.'

They came around a bend in the river and saw the Houseboat up ahead. It had snagged on something. A huge rock. And the force of the water had tipped the Houseboat up on a 45-degree angle. The girls' bedrooms were half under water and the boys' bedroom was high up in the air. Beyond the Houseboat there was another fifty metres of river before it suddenly dropped away over the side of the waterfall.

'Someone will have to go back to camp and tell the counsellors what's happened,' said Patel.

'They won't be any help,' said Friday. 'They're never around when you need them.'

'So what are we going to do?' asked Melanie.

'There's a winch in the storeroom,' said Friday. 'I should know, it's what I sit on every time I'm peeling potatoes. We'll use that and a rope to pull the Houseboat off the rock. Then we can start the engine and sail her back up the river.'

'That doesn't sound easy,' said Melanie.

'Especially in the dark,' said Harvey.

'Then let's get moving before it's pitch-black,' said Friday.

It took ten minutes to gather the equipment. Friday grabbed a life vest as well, just to be on the safe side. One end of the rope was to be fixed to the winch, and the other end was tied around Friday, or rather, around the life vest.

'I'll just jump in upstream and let the current pull me towards the boat,' said Friday.

'If I didn't know you weren't an idiot,' said Melanie, 'I would say that sounds like a pretty idiotic thing to do.'

'Smart people do idiotic things all the time,' said Friday. 'It's because they think they're too smart to be an idiot that is their downfall. I'll be fine, so long as you don't let go of the rope. You can pull me back if I miss the boat.' She waded out into the water.

'I can't believe she's actually doing it,' whispered Susan.

Friday bobbed down in the water as the current caught her and swept her off her feet.

'I'm fine,' called Friday, waving her arm to reassure the rest of her team.

They all waved back. Friday thought this was nice for a millisecond before her brain registered – they were *all* waving.

'One of you needs to grab the rope!' cried Friday.

On the bank, it was hard to hear over the sound of the pounding waterfall.

'What did she say?' asked Melanie.

'One of us needs to have hope?' suggested Wai-Yi.

'That doesn't make sense,' said Patel. 'Surely we should all have hope.'

'Maybe she said, "One of you needs to call the Pope"?' said Harvey.

'But the Pope lives in Italy,' said Susan. 'He'd probably be in bed right now.'

'And I doubt he'd take our call,' said Melanie.

Suddenly the tail end of the rope whipped through the groups' legs and splashed into the river.

'Grab the rope!' cried Patel. 'She said, "Grab the rope"!'

Melanie leapt forward and dived into the river.

'Oh no,' said Susan. 'Now Melanie is going to drown too!'

Melanie was underwater for what seemed like a long time, then she burst through the surface. 'Got it!' she cried happily, holding up the tail end of the rope.

Harvey waded in and grabbed Melanie by the hand, helping her out of the river.

Friday was watching her friends tie the rope to the winch, so she didn't notice that she had reached the Houseboat until she slammed into the back of it.

'I really need to cut down on the number of head injuries I get,' Friday muttered to herself as she rubbed the sore spot.

The water was pushing her hard against the underside of the boat. She had to be careful or she would be pulled beneath it. Friday gripped the timber and dragged herself around to the side. She was glad she had worn the life vest. Swimming was never easy. Particularly after a long day of playing weird sports.

Friday clambered on board. She managed to untie the rope from the life vest, but it took a while because her fingers were cold and slippery. Then she had to retie it to the gunwale. Once she was sure it was secure, she waved to her friends on the bank. She couldn't really see them because her eyesight was terrible, but she was hoping one of them could see her.

Friday turned and started making her way to the engine room. Everything was wet and on a steep slope, so it was like walking up a hill. When she got to the engine room she yanked open the door and stepped inside, bracing herself against the wall to stay upright. It was only now, as she was looking at the internal combustion engine in front of her, that Friday realised it may not go if it was on such an extreme angle. The fluids in the engine may be sitting in the wrong place to get the engine started.

'*Gluteus maximus*,' said Friday. She didn't normally like to swear, but when circumstances made it impossible to avoid she preferred to do it in Latin.

Suddenly there was a dreadful creaking sound and the whole boat began to move.

'Oh no!' exclaimed Friday.

She scrambled to the door, planning to leap free of the boat before it went over the waterfall. But as she got to the doorway, she could see the rope was taut, stretching out to the bank. The rope creaked under the strain. Her friends had done it. They had the winch working. That meant they were pulling the boat upright.

Unfortunately, it took Friday's brain longer to realise this than it took the winch to perform the task. The boat tipped over the balance point and suddenly dropped onto the surface of the water, knocking Friday flat on the deck of the boat. There was a shooting pain through Friday's nose. But she would have to worry about that later. Friday struggled to her feet and hurried to the old diesel engine. She pulled out the choke, and revved it hard. The engine sputtered reluctantly.

'Come on,' Friday pleaded. She wasn't normally one for talking to inanimate objects, but in this case it seemed to work because the engine roared to life. She grabbed the rudder and began steering the boat back up the river. It was working! Friday checked the instruments. The boat was old, but the engine was simple. There wasn't much that could go wrong. Except . . .

Friday noticed the fuel gauge. The tank was practically empty.

'Think!' she urged herself. 'A diesel engine can run on almost any type of oil. There must be some oil on the boat somewhere.'

Friday suddenly remembered Patel's hair oil. She ran around to the boys' room. It was in chaos, but there amongst the mess on the floor was a half-litre bottle of revitalising hair oil. Friday snatched it up and ran to the engine room, where she tipped it into the thirsty machine.

'I hope this works,' she muttered.

She listened anxiously to the note of the motor as the oil drained into the tank.

There was a sputter. Friday held her breath. Then the motor started running again – much more smoothly.

Friday looked at the empty bottle of hair oil in her hand. 'Who would have thought that such a wildly overpriced hair product would make such good motor oil,' she said.

Chapter 18

What Happened?

By the time Friday motored the Houseboat back to its proper mooring, word had got around camp of what was going on. So all the students had gathered along the bank to watch. Some of them still were eating the remnants of their dinner. The dinner the Houseboaters had missed out on.

'Are you all right?' called Melanie as Friday came out of the engine room to throw the tow rope around the bollard.

'Fine,' said Friday. 'A bit cold, but I'll be all right after I dry out.'

'What happened?' asked Ian. He had come down to watch, like all the others.

'Someone cut the rope,' said Friday.

'Are you sure it didn't just snap?' asked Ian. 'Everything around here is pretty old and decrepit.'

Friday held up the end of the rope. 'It's not a clean cut. It took a few hacks, but that's definitely not natural wear and tear.'

'But who would do such a thing?' asked Susan.

'It's pretty extreme,' added Harvey.

'Lots of people don't like us,' said Patel.

'I don't know,' said Friday, 'most people don't think about us much. They may have contempt for us, but this takes real spite. They literally would have had to go out of their way with an axe to do it. I think there is another motive here. There must be a reason they threw all those things in the river as well. We should investigate the scene of the crime.'

'You want to investigate the waterfall?' said Melanie. 'That sounds a bit dangerous.'

'No, I mean inside the Houseboat,' said Friday.

'That's a better idea,' agreed Melanie. 'There are beds in there. I could lie down while you look around.'

The exhausted Houseboaters trooped inside. It was a mess. The common room looked like it had been turned over. Anything that could roll or slide was heaped up against the wall from where the Houseboat had been tipped up near the waterfall. Patel emerged from the boys' room.

'Everything is okay in here,' he said. 'Although my hair oil is missing from the bathroom.'

Friday went over to see. The room looked like an explosive device had gone off inside it. Clothes and possessions were strewn everywhere.

'But it's been ransacked,' said Friday.

Harvey peered into the room. 'No, this is what it always looks like.'

'Melanie, how's our room?' Friday called across to her friend, who she'd seen disappear into their room moments earlier. There was no response. Friday walked over. Melanie was fast asleep on her bed already.

'Three seconds!' exclaimed Friday. 'She went from walking to asleep in three seconds. That must be a new record, even for Melanie.'

'To be fair,' said Patel, 'it has been a long day.'

Friday looked about at their room. It had been jumbled about, but everything still seemed to be there. Melanie and Friday hadn't really brought much with them, except books, and it was unlikely anyone would want to steal those.

'You'd better come and see our room,' called Wai-Yi.

Friday headed over to the other girls' room. There was nothing to see. Apart from the beds, the room had been completely stripped bare.

'I guess that explains all the stuff floating in the river,' said Friday. 'Don't worry, you can borrow our spare clothes.'

Wai-Yi and Susan exchanged a look.

'You can borrow Melanie's spare clothes,' said Friday.

Wai-Yi and Susan smiled. 'No offence, Friday,' said Susan. 'You know we love you. We just don't think we could pull off a brown cardigan as well as you can.'

'Now we've got a mystery to solve. Somebody came on board and threw all your stuff out the window,' said Friday, 'then used an axe to cut the whole Houseboat adrift and let it float down the river and over a waterfall. Do either of you have any enemies?'

Wai-Yi and Susan shook their heads.

'Are you sure?' asked Friday. 'Because it's such a specific time to do it. There was such a small window of opportunity while we were at the medal presentation ceremony. Are you certain you didn't make any enemies sometime in the last two hours?'

'It was Drake!' Melanie called from the other room.

'What?' said Friday.

Melanie sat up and yawned. 'Sorry, I was asleep and my unconscious could still hear you talking.'

'What do you mean it was Drake?' asked Friday.

'You asked if Wai-Yi or Susan upset anyone in the last two hours,' said Melanie.

'But I never upset anyone,' said Wai-Yi. 'That's a big part of why I don't talk to people – I don't want to appear rude.'

'I try to avoid talking too,' added Susan. 'It makes me blush. I can't stop myself. And then my head looks like a beetroot.'

'But when Drake wanted to carry you in the piggyback race, you rebuffed him,' said Melanie, emerging from the bedroom. 'Boys hate that. Especially if they're secretly in love with you. Isn't that right, Ian?'

Ian didn't respond, except to roll his eyes.

'Oh my gosh!' exclaimed Wai-Yi. 'Melanie's right. He gave you a rock!'

'What?' asked Friday. 'Do you have a shared interest in geology?'

'No, we were making pet rocks in bushcraft class,' explained Susan.

'This camp has the strangest ways of teaching wilderness survival skills,' said Friday.

'Drake was at the table next to us,' said Wai-Yi, 'and when he finished, he gave Susan his rock.'

'I didn't think anything of it at the time,' said Susan. 'I just assumed he didn't want it.'

'Where's the rock now?' asked Friday.

'You remember how the toilet wasn't flushing?' said Susan. 'It's because the handle wasn't balanced properly.'

'Susan's father has a plumbing empire,' explained Wai-Yi.

'I stuck the rock in the cistern to hold the valve in place,' said Susan.

'Let's have a look,' said Friday.

They all went to the bathroom. Friday tried to get the lid off the cistern, but then stood back and let Susan do it because she was clearly the expert.

'Here it is,' said Susan as she reached in and fished out a wet rock. It had googly eyes and wet wool glued to the top.

'Oh, how sweet,' said Melanie. 'It's actually rather cute for a rock.'

'But it's still just a rock, not a motive,' said Friday, peering closely at the pet rock's face. She turned it over in her hand. 'Hang on a minute. Look at this . . .'

There were three symbols painted on the underside.

'What is that?' asked Ian, peering over Friday's shoulder.

'It looks like an archery target, a love heart and a rain cloud,' said Susan.

'Is it some sort of coded message?' asked Melanie.

'Yes, it is,' said Friday. 'Is Drake any good at art?'

'Not really,' said Susan. 'That pet rock didn't look much better before I put it in the cistern.'

'Then I know what this is saying,' said Friday. 'The archery target isn't a target. It's an eye. The inner circle is the pupil, the middle circle is the retina and the outer circle is the white of the eye.'

'Then what's the love heart?' asked Ian.

'A love heart,' said Friday.

'And the rain cloud?' asked Melanie.

'I don't think it's a rain cloud,' said Friday. 'I think it's meant to be a drawing of a woolly sheep.'

'I love sheep,' said Melanie. 'But that's a strange message to give a girl.'

'A female sheep is called a "ewe",' said Friday. 'He's saying, "I love ewe" or rather "I love you".'

'That's so romantic!' said Melanie. 'Slightly confusing, but very romantic. You should give Friday a rock like that, Ian.'

Susan took the rock from Friday's hand. 'So are you saying that Drake likes me and that's why he ransacked our room and set the Houseboat floating down the river?'

'Yes,' said Friday. 'When you rebuffed him, he must have panicked and thought you didn't like him, then panicked more because he'd given you this rock, so he was desperate to get rid of it before you realised what the message said. So he sabotaged his own team by crashing into Ian and me in the piggy-back race. Then while we were celebrating our victory and everyone was distracted, he raced down to the Houseboat to retrieve the rock.'

'But that's so extreme,' said Ian.

'Teenage boys are hormonal, their brains process information differently to regular humans,' said Friday. 'They're impulsive and extreme.'

'I told you it was romantic,' said Melanie.

'He threw all of our stuff into the river. Then when he couldn't find the rock, he got desperate and set the Houseboat adrift,' said Susan.

'Yeah, but he gave you a very sweet rock,' said Wai-Yi.

'The course of true love never did run smooth,' said Melanie.

'Are you quoting Shakespeare now?' asked Friday.

'Just because I sleep through most of English, doesn't mean I don't pick up on some of the good bits,' said Melanie.

'So what are you going to do?' asked Ian. 'Report him to Geraldine? Or the police?'

'The Houseboat is fine,' said Friday, 'and Susan and Wai-Yi aren't too worried about their stuff. I think Susan should attempt to engage Drake in some sort of social ritual. Whatever the custom for adolescent courting-couples is these days.'

'She could talk to him,' said Melanie.

'There you go,' said Friday. 'Case closed.'

Most of the crowd outside had drifted away, but Drake was still standing on the riverbank. Susan looked terrified.

'Just say the first thing that comes into your head,' said Melanie. 'Unless the first thing is "I'm a serial killer", in which case say something different.' She gave Susan a firm push in Drake's direction.

Susan blushed. Drake stared at the ground and scuffed the dirt with his foot.

'So,' said Susan.

'So,' said Drake.

There was another long pause.

'Do you want to go for a walk with me?' asked Susan. 'I'm going to take a flashlight and go down the river searching for any of my stuff that may have washed up on the bank.'

'Sure!' said Drake. 'Would you like me to carry the flashlight for you?'

'Sure,' said Susan. She handed him the flashlight and they headed off together.

Melanie sighed. 'Why can't you two be so easy to get together?' she asked Friday and Ian.

'At least I don't go around setting houseboats adrift,' said Ian.

'It would be so romantic if you did, though,' said Melanie.

Friday didn't respond. She was too busy staring at the duffel bag by Ian's feet.

'From the I.W. on that bag I deduce that it's yours,' said Friday. 'It's highly unusual to be taking such a large bag for a walk this late at night. Unless it contains some sort of contraband that you're trying to smuggle under the cover of darkness.'

'Nothing that exciting, I'm afraid,' said Ian. 'The bag contains all my worldly possessions. At least, the ones I brought with me to camp.'

'You're taking your belongings for a late-night walk then?' asked Melanie.

'I've been thrown out of the Treehouse,' said Ian. 'The rest of the team had a vote. They're expelling me for losing the final challenge.'

'Why are you here?' asked Friday.

'Oh, Friday,' said Melanie, 'how can you be so obtuse?'

'The Houseboat is the only place with free beds,' said Ian. 'I had to come here. It was either that or build a shelter in the woods, and the counsellors have never gotten around to teaching us how to do that.'

'Welcome!' said Harvey. 'We could do with another boy. Come on, we'll show you where the spare beds are in the boys' room.'

The three boys went back into the Houseboat.

'Well done, Friday!' said Melanie, giving her friend a hug.

'I didn't do anything,' said Friday.

'You tumbled over Ian's head, smashing his face into the ground, which did result in him being here,' said Melanie. 'Maybe on some subconscious level you instinctively knew to do that.'

'Aaaggghhh!' they heard Susan screaming from far away in the forest.

'What was that?' asked Melanie.

'Susan,' said Friday.

They took off running down the bank. But they hadn't gone far when they collided head-on with Susan herself.

'Aaaaggghhh!' said Susan again.

Drake caught up to her and wrapped his arms around her. 'It's all right, you're safe now,' he said.

'What happened?' asked Friday.

'We saw it,' said Drake.

'Saw what?' asked Melanie.

'The ghost of Ghost Mountain!' said Susan before dissolving into sobs and weeping on Drake's chest. He seemed to be quite enjoying the situation.

'Was it an eerie glowing green human shape?' asked Friday.

'Yes!' said Drake. 'How did you know?'

'I've seen it too,' said Friday.

'And you didn't think to mention it before now?' asked Melanie.

'Ghosts don't exist,' said Friday. 'It was far more likely to be an optical hallucination caused by one of the many blows to the head I keep suffering.'

'There's something out there,' said Melanie. 'And it's watching us.'

'It's true,' said Drake. 'Here . . .' He held out a small torn rag. It glowed a strange green colour in the darkness. 'I think this came from the ghost's clothes.'

'Ghosts don't wear clothes,' said Friday.

'Of course they do,' said Melanie. 'Who ever heard of a naked ghost?'

Friday sniffed the rag. 'And this smells funny. This is a very strange ghost.'

Chapter 19

The Final Frontier

'To graduate from Camp Courage, you must pass the final challenge,' said Geraldine.

'Please don't let it be latrine digging, please don't let it be latrine digging,' muttered Patel under his breath.

'And that challenge is ...' Geraldine paused dramatically so that she could relish the moment of dread. 'A three-day wilderness hike to Ghost Mountain and back.'

'How far away is Ghost Mountain?' Melanie whispered to Friday.

'About twenty kilometres,' said Friday.

'That's not too bad,' said Melanie. 'Twenty kilometres in three days.'

'No, twenty kilometres there, plus twenty kilometres back – and a lot of that is uphill, over rocks and crossing rivers and cliffs,' said Friday.

Melanie put her hand up.

'What are you doing?' whispered Friday.

'I'm going to ask a question,' said Melanie.

'Why?' asked Friday. 'It won't go well.'

'What?' Geraldine barked at Melanie.

'What happens if we don't pass the final challenge?' asked Melanie.

Geraldine grinned. 'You have to spend another week at camp.'

'What? Revising survival skills?' asked Melanie.

'Oh, no,' said Geraldine. 'Cleaning up after everyone else has gone. Someone has to fill in the latrines you've dug. Otherwise, how will I punish the next group to come here?'

The students all started muttering amongst themselves.

'You will all head off at dawn tomorrow,' said Geraldine. 'I have mapped out four different routes so that you can't help one another's group while you're out there. The Houseboat team gets first pick of the routes as reward for winning the Colour War.'

'Where will we sleep?' asked Mirabella.

'Under the stars,' said Geraldine.

Mirabella looked confused. 'Is that the name of the hotel where we'll be staying?'

'Duh, we'll be camping,' said Trea Babcock.

'Oh no, you won't,' said Geraldine. 'When you camp, you have a tent. But you won't have tents. You will have a blanket each, and three days' worth of survival rations. If you want shelter, you will have to build it yourself. If you want a proper meal, you will have to find the food yourself.'

'Are we allowed to call tradesmen to come and help?' asked Daisy Jump.

'No,' said Geraldine. 'You can't call a tradesman to come and make a survival shelter for you.'

'That's not fair,' said Daisy. 'That's what I'd do if I was really lost in the wilderness.'

'I'm never going to be lost in the wilderness,' said Trea Babcock. 'I don't plan on ever leaving the urban area again.'

'What if you're in a plane crash over the Amazon jungle?' asked Melanie.

'Daddy's pilot has never had a crash,' said Trea.

'Enough!' snapped Geraldine. 'Go and get ready. You are leaving at 7 am tomorrow.'

'Nooooooo!' cried Melanie, leaping to her feet and lunging for Geraldine. Friday grabbed her by the waist before she could attack her. 'Anything but an early morning. Please, please, I'll do anything!'

'You lot need to get tough,' said Geraldine. 'In three days' time, you will be.'

Chapter 20

Surviving

'Wake up, wake up, girls!' yelled Sebastian. 'It's time to go.'

Friday opened her eyes and looked at her alarm clock. 'But it's only 5 o'clock.' She rolled over and glanced at the window. 'And it's dark outside.'

'It's Geraldine's idea,' explained Sebastian, calling through the door. 'She says you need to learn night navigation, so you might as well start off with that.'

Several minutes later, the bleary-eyed students gathered on the riverbank next to the jetty.

'Okay, we're all here,' said Sebastian. 'I've packed seven backpacks for you. Each contains three days' worth of survival rations and blankets. You're not allowed to take anything else.'

Susan put up her hand. 'What about clean underwear?'

'You're meant to wear the same underwear for three days,' said Sebastian.

Susan and Wai-Yi gasped.

'That does not sound hygienic,' said Patel.

'This is meant to be a wilderness survival challenge,' said Sebastian. 'Nothing we are about to do in the next three days will be hygienic. Although, if you can figure out how to fashion a clean pair of underpants out of leaves and twigs, I suppose I can allow that. Come on, let's go before Geraldine realises we're still here and comes down to yell at us.'

'I've got something to say!' declared Melanie.

Everyone turned to look at her. They hadn't thought she was properly awake yet, because she had been standing very still with her eyes closed.

'It's not too late,' said Melanie. 'Normally I don't approve of running, but if we start now we could make a run for it and try to escape.'

'It'll be fine,' said Friday. 'We're just going to go walking for three days. It's not a big deal. We were able to pick the easiest route. We've got food. It'll be quite nice. There will be wildflowers, birds to listen to and no electric lighting, so as soon as it gets dark we can go to sleep.'

'I guess,' said Melanie begrudgingly.

'Come on,' said Ian. 'If we start now, we can get the first few kilometres in before we wake up properly.'

The group set out. They were all supposed to be learning how to navigate, so Patel was in charge of the map for the first stage, under Sebastian's supervision.

'It looks pretty simple,' said Patel, staring closely at the map in the pale moonlight. 'I think we just need to walk up the river for about five centimetres until we come to a bridge.'

'Five *kilometres*,' said Friday. 'The map is a one to one thousand scale. Each centimetre represents a kilometre.'

'Yes, well, you knew what I meant,' said Patel. 'This way.' He turned and began walking.

'I thought you said we had to walk north along the river?' said Friday.

'Yes,' said Patel.

'That way is south,' said Friday.

'Are you sure?' asked Patel.

'The sun has risen on the far side of the bank and has set on this side of the bank every day that we've been here, so yes,' said Friday.

'Okay,' said Patel. 'Then let's go this way.'

The group turned and started trudging upstream.

'I'm going back to sleep,' muttered Melanie.

'You can't, we have to start hiking,' said Friday.

'Hmmph, I can do both at the same time,' said Melanie grumpily.

It took two hours to reach the bridge. They would have arrived sooner, but Patel had gotten lost while taking a toilet break and it took twenty minutes for the group to find him again. Fortunately, Friday had researched how to track an animal through the undergrowth, and it was particularly easy when that animal was crashing about in circles, knocking down branches and stumbling over rocks.

'Are you sure this bridge is safe?' asked Susan.

It did look very rickety. It was just a footbridge. The supports were all rope, and the treads were timber slats. The slats looked like they had been there for a hundred years. And a hundred years in damp conditions with insects and microbes eating away at it had clearly had an effect.

'There's one way to find out,' said Friday.

'Send Patel across first and see if he falls through into the river?' asked Ian.

'Okay, there are *two* ways to find out,' said Friday as she picked up a large stone, went over to the foot of the bridge and tossed the stone as far as she could onto the walkway.

The rock landed with a thud onto a slat. The whole bridge wobbled but held firm.

'There, you see,' said Sebastian. 'Perfectly fine.'

Sebastian stepped onto the bridge and immediately his leg crashed through the first timber slat, his foot dangling down in the water. Ian and Harvey rushed forward to help him out.

'Okay, some of the timbers may be a little weak,' conceded Sebastian, 'but if you hold onto the handrails with both hands, I'm sure you'll be fine.'

'Come on,' said Ian, striding onto the bridge, 'what's the big deal? If we do fall in, we can all swim, can't we?' He walked confidently across, not even bothering to touch the handrails.

'I can swim in a swimming pool when it's heated, with lane markers and no rocks, currents or undertow,' said Harvey. 'I don't fancy taking a dip in this river.'

'Then you better hang on tight,' said Friday. She followed after Ian. Although she did hold onto the handrails, just in case.

Eventually the whole group got across with only minimal weeping from Patel, when he got a blister on his hand from clutching the handrail a little too enthusiastically.

'Who's going to take the map next?' asked Sebastian. No one volunteered.

'Okay, Harvey, it's your turn,' decided Sebastian.

'But I'm as blind as a bat,' said Harvey.

'Actually, most bats have good vision,' said Friday. 'It would be better to say something like "My eyes are as blind as the eyes of a potato".'

'You've got potatoes on the brain from too much time peeling,' said Melanie.

'Harvey, just have your turn now, before we get too far from base camp,' said Sebastian. 'In case you get us lost.'

Harvey took the map and held it so close to his face that it looked as if he was sniffing it, not reading it.

Sebastian handed him the compass. 'This will help.'

Harvey glanced between the map and the compass several times before making a decision. 'This way.' He pointed out a path that led up to the mountain and the group started off again.

They hadn't been walking for long when it started to rain.

'Shouldn't we stop and build a shelter?' asked Ian.

'It's just drizzle,' said Sebastian. 'We need to cover as much distance as we can while we have daylight.'

'But isn't staying dry one of the first principles of wilderness survival?' asked Friday.

'Oh yes, of course,' said Sebastian, 'but this is just a passing shower. We'll dry off as we walk.'

As it turned out, Sebastian was entirely wrong. They walked for three hours, and the rain just got heavier and heavier. Soon it was raining so hard they could barely see twenty metres in front of them. They couldn't hear each other without yelling because the rain was beating down on the forest foliage so loudly. But worst of all, it got very slippery. The path they were following was a combination of dirt and rock. As the rain grew ever heavier, the dirt turned to mud and the rocks became slick. Melanie was the first to lose her footing. Luckily she fell backwards into Harvey and he caught her, otherwise she would have tumbled down the path.

'We need to find shelter!' Friday yelled at Sebastian.

'What?' asked Sebastian, cupping his hand to his ear.

'We need to get out of the rain,' said Friday. 'Before someone gets hurt.'

'I know,' said Sebastian. 'Up ahead there's a place called Whale Rock Cave. If we make it there, we won't have to build a shelter. Then we can start a fire and dry our clothes out.'

'How much further is this cave?' asked Ian. 'It's starting to get dangerous out here. This path is turning into a waterslide.'

'It should take us about half an hour to get there, if we push hard,' said Sebastian, checking the map.

'Okay, let's get going,' said Ian. 'Melanie, give me your bag. I'll carry it for you.'

'I'll be okay,' said Melanie.

'I'm not offering to be kind,' said Ian. 'I'm offering to carry your bag so that I don't have to carry you if the extra weight of your bag makes you slip and topple over.'

Melanie handed over her bag and they all continued walking.

Under unpleasant conditions, the smallest amount of time can seem to drag forever. But this is especially so when it actually does drag forever. They were still trudging uphill through torrential rain and mud sixty minutes later.

'Where is this cave?' called Friday.

'We must be nearly there,' said Sebastian.

They kept walking for another twenty minutes. Sebastian was striding ahead at the front of the group, so it was hard to talk to him. Friday tried catching up with him, but her much-shorter legs couldn't do it. In the end, she picked up a small rock and threw it at his backpack. Luckily she hit it first time.

'Hey!' cried Sebastian, spinning around. 'Who did that?'

'I did!' Friday yelled over the sound of the rain. 'Are we lost?'

'Of course not,' said Sebastian. 'We just have to go up here a bit further.'

'Are you sure?' asked Friday.

'In the wilderness, a group has to trust their leader,' said Sebastian. 'Chain of command is important for morale. We have to keep walking because I say so, now come on.'

Friday sat down on a rock. The others started trudging after Sebastian. As Harvey passed her, she grabbed his sleeve.

'Harvey, can you show me the map, please,' said Friday.

Harvey didn't argue. He just handed it over. Friday studied it as the rest of the group kept walking.

'Stop!' cried Friday.

They all halted. Several of them sat down where they were in the pouring rain.

'We can't stop moving!' yelled Sebastian as he stomped back down the track towards Friday. 'They'll all get hypothermia if they don't keep exercising until we get out of the rain.'

'I understand the body's response to extreme cold and exhaustion,' said Friday. 'I'm telling you to stop, because you're going the wrong way.'

'Friday, Sebastian is a professional wilderness survival instructor,' said Ian. 'I'm sure he knows the way to the cave. We don't have time for your theatrics. We have to keep moving.'

'But it's right here on the map,' said Friday. 'We've been walking south-west at a gradient of thirty degrees for the last two hours. We're going very slowly, so we'd be covering about four kilometres an hour. That puts us here.'

Friday pointed to a spot on the map.

'But the Whale Rock Cave is over here,' continued Friday, pointing to another spot on the map. 'We should have been heading south-east. The cave is four kilometres away, in that direction. We've been travelling on the wrong tangent.'

'Are you sure?' asked Ian.

'Sebastian has been guiding us south-*west*,' said Friday. 'He's been taking us in entirely the wrong direction.'

Sebastian took the map from Friday and studied it. It was pouring with rain and there wasn't much light under the forest canopy, but he appeared to turn pale. He looked up, glancing all around.

'You're looking for landmarks, aren't you?' said Friday.

Sebastian ignored her.

'There aren't any,' said Friday. 'At least none we can see.'

'Are you sure about this?' asked Ian.

'Yes,' said Friday.

'We've got no way of checking,' said Ian. 'We can't even see the sun to use that as a guide.'

Friday took the compass from Harvey. 'Look, that way is due north. We've been walking from that direction, north-east.' She pointed at the long path that stretched behind them. 'So we've been walking south-west. It's simple.'

Ian turned to Sebastian. 'How could you make a stuff-up like that? You've put our lives in danger.'

'If we keep walking this way, I'm sure we'll come to shelter,' said Sebastian, looking back up the path.

'Can you get us to that cave?' Ian asked Friday.

Friday looked at the map. 'Yes, but it will take us at least an hour and a half to get there. Longer, if the weather doesn't improve.'

'Come on, then, we'd better get moving,' said Ian. 'Friday, you keep the map. You're in charge of navigating now. No offence, Harvey.'

'None taken,' said Harvey. 'I'm glad not to have the responsibility.'

'Susan, Wai-Yi, I'll carry your bags for you,' said Harvey, 'if you hold onto my hands and make sure I don't get lost. I'm finding it harder and harder to see.'

'Good idea,' said Ian. 'Come on, let's go.'

The group headed out, following Friday. Sebastian didn't argue. He wanted to get out of the rain too.

It was a horrible hour and a half. The weather did not let up. And they were all exhausted. Plus, their wet clothes had started to chafe, so they were uncomfortable in every possible way, and in every possible place.

But they must have gained some fitness over the past four weeks of woodchopping and latrine digging, because somehow they were all able to keep trudging forward.

It was just starting to get dark when Friday called out.

'Over there!' she cried.

Up ahead was a large rock that clearly looked like a whale. And underneath the rock was a ledge that provided a natural cave shelter.

The group hurried forward. Sebastian had been lagging further and further behind. He ran to catch up now.

Patel was the first to reach the cave. 'Thank goodness!' he said as he dropped his bag on the dry floor and collapsed. Ian, Susan, Wai-Yi and Harvey were close behind. Friday took Melanie by the hand and helped her the last few metres. Melanie grabbed Friday in a hug. 'Thank you, thank you so much.'

'What for?' asked Friday, hugging her friend back. She didn't often get to hug people, but she was so exhausted, she was too tired to feel uncomfortable.

'For being the sort of weirdo who knows how to read a map and use a compass even in a rainstorm,' said Melanie.

'You're welcome,' said Friday.

'Here comes Sebastian,' said Ian. 'He's got some explaining to do. I don't understand how he could make such a big mistake.'

'Everyone makes mistakes,' said Friday.

Her words turned out to be instantly prophetic. Sebastian was jogging up the hill towards the cave, when the rocks under his foot slid out from under him and his forward momentum, combined with the bag he was carrying, threw him forward, crunching his forehead down on a large rock.

Susan screamed, 'Aaaaaggghh!' Then when everyone looked at her she apologised. 'Sorry, it just seemed like an appropriate response.'

Ian and Friday hurried out into the rain to help Sebastian. Friday didn't need to check his pulse, because he groaned. 'Well, he's alive,' she said.

Ian rolled Sebastian over and as he did they could see blood pouring from Sebastian's scalp.

Friday instantly fainted.

Chapter 21

No Return

When Friday woke up she was lying on the floor of the cave. She looked across to see Melanie binding a bandage around Sebastian's head. Friday reached up and touched her own head. There was a bandage there too. Which would explain her splitting headache.

'You hit your head on a rock when you fainted,' said Ian. 'It was my fault. If I'd been more on the ball, I would have realised that was how you would react to the sight of blood and caught you.'

'Is Sebastian okay?' asked Friday.

'He's fine. Just a bump on the head and a sprained ankle,' said Ian. 'But I'm going to kill him when we get back to camp.'

'We need a fire,' said Friday. 'We need to get dry and warm. It'll be dark soon and the temperature will drop.'

'We can't light a fire,' said Ian. 'We've got no kindling, no matches and, with everything wet, there is no way we're going to start a fire by rubbing two sticks together.'

'No,' agreed Friday, 'but if you find the driest wood you can get, looking under old logs and around the mouth of the cave, then we should be able to get one started using the lighter I smuggled along in the secret pocket in my sock.'

Friday pulled up her trouser leg, unzipped the pocket on her sock and pulled out a gas lighter.

'I could kiss you,' said Ian.

'Please do,' said Melanie. 'This is all very grim, and some romance would cheer me up.'

'A fire would cheer you up more,' said Friday. 'Go on, see what you can find.' She lay back and closed her eyes while the others began searching.

A few minutes later they had a decent collection. 'It's all a bit damp,' said Ian, 'but a couple of the logs are surprisingly dry. The fire should be all right if we can get it started.'

'We don't have any tinder,' said Patel.

'Do we have anything in our backpacks that we could use?' asked Friday. 'Any cloth or paper?'

'No,' said Ian. 'The food is all stored in plastic or aluminium containers. And the blankets are made of wool, which is flame-retardant.'

'And none of our clothes are dry enough to use,' said Patel.

'Does anyone have any paper?' asked Friday.

Everyone shook their heads, except Melanie.

'You do,' said Melanie. 'The map.'

'We can't burn that,' said Ian. 'It's our way out of here.'

'We won't need a map to get us out of here if we don't survive the night,' said Friday.

'But we need a map,' said Ian.

'Not if I memorise it first,' said Friday.

'You can do that?' asked Susan.

'Do you have a photographic memory?' asked Wai-Yi.

234

'No one has photographic memory. It's a popular culture myth,' said Friday. 'Eidetic memory exists in a small percentage of young children. But at twelve, I'm on the cusp of being too old even for that. I merely have a very good memory, as well as excellent concentration and mental discipline. But I believe that will be enough.' She took the map out of its protective pouch, unfolded it to its full size and methodically studied it from one corner to the other. Then she squinted and rubbed her forehead. 'Of course, normally, I don't have a head injury.'

'You do get them quite a lot,' said Melanie. 'I'm sure you can do it.'

Friday silently stared at the map, taking it all in. 'Okay, let's start the fire.' She tore the map in half and started scrunching it up.

'This feels so wrong,' said Ian.

'I know,' said Friday, 'but you'll feel better about it when we get a fire going.'

Friday arranged the scrunched-up balls of paper on the ground, then started laying twigs, sticks and eventually logs over the top.

'We've only got one shot at this,' said Ian. 'Good luck.'

Friday lay down on the floor, held the lighter to the paper and flicked it on.

The paper caught quickly and flared up. The flames spread throughout the dry paper. Moisture hissed off the damp twigs.

'Do you think they're dry enough to catch light?' asked Ian.

'We'll soon see,' said Friday. She started to blow gently on the fire to encourage the flame to flare up.

'Not too much,' warned Ian.

'I know the principles of fire lighting,' said Friday.

'Just because you know the principles in theory, doesn't mean you know how to do it in practice,' said Ian.

'It's better than knowing nothing,' said Friday.

'It's lit!' exclaimed Melanie.

Friday and Ian turned from their argument to see the first of the twigs start to take flame. Friday leaned down and blew gently. The flames spread to the other twigs.

'I can't believe it,' said Ian. 'It's working.'

Soon they had a roaring fire. There was a lot of smoke because of the dampness of the wood, but they didn't care. If they lay on the floor the smoke rose away. And they made makeshift coathangers out of branches and hung their clothes over the flames to dry them out. Patel did accidentally set fire to his shirt. But he didn't set fire to his pants, so it was only moderately embarrassing.

As the sun rose the following morning, the House-boaters hadn't had much sleep. But they'd had some, their clothes were largely dry and they'd eaten well. As a group, they had decided to eat most of their supplies. They should be back at Camp Courage by mid-afternoon and if they ate them now, it would mean less to carry. Which was no small consideration because they were going to have to carry Sebastian.

His ankle had gotten a lot worse during the night. It had swollen up to twice its natural size. And by the morning light, they could see it had gone a spectacular shade of purple as well.

'Is it broken?' asked Sebastian as Friday examined it.

'I don't know,' said Friday. 'It's your ankle. What do you think?'

'It feels broken,' said Sebastian.

'There's no bone sticking through the skin,' said Friday, 'so that's a good thing.'

'You don't have very good bedside manner, you know,' said Sebastian.

'All the doctors in my family are doctors of physics,' said Friday. 'They don't have any bedside manner at all.'

'How are we going to carry him all the way back to camp?' asked Patel.

'It took us twelve hours to walk here,' said Harvey. 'If we have to carry Sebastian, it will take longer to get back.'

'No, it won't,' said Friday. 'We'll be able to cut four hours off our time by not getting lost, for a start. Plus, we'll be walking downhill, so it will be easier.'

'And the rain has eased up,' said Melanie. 'It's only light rain now, as opposed to the torrential rain we had yesterday.'

'We could just stay put and wait for help to arrive,' said Susan.

'It will be another thirty-six hours before we're expected back,' said Ian. 'Then they'll probably wait another twelve hours in case we are just late. So it would be two days before they start looking for us.'

'It won't be so bad,' said Friday. 'We can make a sled out of branches and a blanket, and drag him. We can chuck our backpacks on the sled as well and take turns pulling it.'

The sled was a little trickier to make than Friday had first imagined. Sebastian fell straight through the first two prototypes, hitting his head on the ground, then on another rock, which only increased his whining. But the third attempt worked much better and by 7 am they were able to set out into the rain, going back down the hill.

It was a grim walk but not as horrible as the day before, because at least this time Friday was in charge of navigation so they had every confidence they were heading in the right direction.

It took them just three hours to make it back to the river.

'Woohoo!' cried Ian as he broke through the tree line and saw the roaring river ahead. 'We made it!'

As the rest of the group joined him on the bank, there was lots of high-fiving, hugs and slaps on the back. Even Sebastian looked slightly less miserable.

'You did it, Friday,' said Patel. 'Well done!'

But Friday was not sharing in the jubilation. She was looking up and down the river.

'What's wrong?' asked Melanie. 'Don't tell me this is the wrong river, and we've ended up in Timbuctoo.'

'Oh no, this is the right river,' said Friday. 'The problem is, there's no bridge.'

The mood suddenly soured.

'What are you talking about?' said Ian. 'We've probably just come out of the forest a bit upstream. If we follow the river a little way, we'll come to it.'

Friday shook her head. 'The bridge should be right there.' She pointed to a spot directly in front of them.

'You must have made a mistake,' said Ian. 'You're not perfect, you know.'

'I may make mistakes about social conventions and fashion choices, but map reading is essentially just applied mathematics using trigonometry and ratios, and I *do not* make mistakes in mathematics,' said Friday, walking closer to the raging river.

'Don't get too close,' warned Melanie.

Friday stood right on the edge and peered into the water. She crouched down, reached into the water and pulled out a rope. 'This is the handrail. The rest of the bridge must have been swept away by the floodwater.'

Someone started sobbing. Friday looked about and was surprised to see it was Sebastian.

'It's probably the pain,' said Friday.

'No,' said Melanie, 'I think it's because he's a big wimp.'

'What are we going to do?' asked Ian. 'We've got no way back, we've eaten most of our food and we burned our map.'

'We could cook and eat Sebastian,' said Melanie.

Sebastian wailed.

'I didn't mean it,' said Melanie. 'I just wanted to see how he would react. He didn't surprise me.'

'We could cross the river,' said Patel. 'It's only fifty metres to swim.'

'Fifty metres in a raging current, with who-knows-what storm damage floating in the water,' said Ian. 'It would be too dangerous.'

'The next bridge is fourteen kilometres down-stream,' said Friday.

'Fourteen kilometres!' said Wai-Yi. 'I can't hike that far. My blisters have blisters already!'

'It's fourteen kilometres if you follow the river,' said Friday, 'but the river bends. It would only be nine kilometres if we went through the forest.'

'We don't all have to go,' said Ian. 'Friday and I will hike out. The rest of you should stay here with Sebastian. Use fallen branches to build a shelter. When we get back to camp, we'll send help for you.'

'What if you don't get back?' asked Wai-Yi.

'Then you're better off without us,' said Ian.

'I'll leave my lighter for you,' said Friday, 'so you can start a fire.'

'I'm going with you two,' said Melanie.

'Are you sure?' asked Friday.

'I don't like being left behind,' said Melanie. 'I find it hard to follow what's going on when you're not around. Plus, I don't mind walking. So long as I don't have to run, I'll be okay.'

'Let's get going then,' said Ian, 'before it starts to rain. Which way do we go?'

Friday pointed out across the tree line. 'That way,' she said.

'No!' cried Sebastian. He rolled over onto his knees and, using a stick as a crutch, struggled up onto his one good foot. 'I forbid it. I am the adult here. I won't let you go off on your own.'

'Why not?' asked Ian.

'It's not safe,' said Sebastian. 'You'll get lost.'

'I've got the compass,' said Friday, holding it up in her hand. 'If we head twelve degrees north by north-east, we can't get lost.'

Sebastian swung his crutch up quickly and smacked Friday hard on the underside of the hand.

'Oww!' cried Friday.

The compass flew up. Sebastian dived for it. And so did Ian. But Sebastian got there first. He wrenched the compass away from Ian and threw it with all his might into the surging river. The compass landed with a plop and was quickly swept away.

'What did you do that for?' demanded Ian.

'To stop you doing something stupid!' yelled Sebastian. 'Now you'll have to stay here.'

Chapter 22

Something Nasty

'I can still navigate using what little we can see of the sun and the stars,' said Friday. 'And if need be, I can make another compass with a magnet, a pin and a leaf. You've just made it harder, that's all.'

'I'm ordering you to stay here!' demanded Sebastian.

'We're not staying here with you,' said Ian. 'Lemmings have better survival skills than you do.

Let's go. Harvey, if he gives you any trouble while we're gone, just bop him on the head with a rock.'

'I might bop him on the head right now just to save time,' muttered Harvey.

As Friday, Ian and Melanie headed off, Sebastian was still ranting behind them.

'Come back! Come back, now!'

'What's all that about?' wondered Ian.

'His ankle is probably hurting so much it makes him feel emotional,' said Melanie.

'I think he's upset about something more than that,' said Friday, glancing back.

They were only hiking for another hour when the sun broke out.

'Hooray!' said Ian. 'At last.'

'That's going to make it easier to navigate too,' said Friday, glancing at the sun then her wristwatch. 'You can work out which way is north by pointing the twelve on your watch at the sun, then halving the distance to the hour hand.'

Melanie looked over her shoulder. 'You're wearing a digital watch.'

'I can imagine where an hour hand would be on an analog watch,' said Friday.

'Really?' said Melanie. 'I always find proper watches very confusing, even when they're not imaginary.'

'This way,' said Friday.

They pushed through the scrub, and trudged over the top of a small hill when suddenly in the middle of the forest they came across a big tin shed.

'Civilisation!' cried Melanie.

They all hurried forward. But as they drew close, they noticed something odd about the building.

'What is that noise?' asked Ian.

'What's that smell?' asked Melanie.

'Let's take a look,' said Friday, stretching up on tippy-toes to peer in through the window. The glass was filthy and covered in cobwebs. She smeared the dirt away with the cuff of her sleeve. Ian and Melanie joined her to peer through.

The shed was full of cages, stacked four high, and in long rows stretching from one end of the shed to the other. In the cages were small furry animals.

'Are they ferrets?' asked Ian.

'I know some people like ferrets as pets,' said Melanie, 'but there must be hundreds in there. That's a lot of pets.'

'They're not ferrets,' said Friday. 'A ferret is a domesticated form of European polecat. Those are minks. They're the same genus, but they're not domesticated. They're highly aggressive.'

'Why would someone keep a shed full of minks in the middle of nowhere?' asked Ian.

'For their fur,' said Friday. 'Mink is one of the most highly sought-after pelts in the fur trade.'

'But nobody wears fur anymore,' said Melanie. 'One of Mummy's friends wore a fur stole to their Aspen ski party, and she was thrown out of the bridge club and the light opera society.'

'They do in Eastern Europe and Canada,' said Friday. 'Mink is still one the best ways to stay warm in extremely cold temperatures.'

'But why keep minks out here?' asked Ian.

'It's brilliant,' said Friday. 'It's so isolated. It's close to the river. They could take the minks out on a boat. No one would ever know they were here.'

'Who would do such a thing?' asked Melanie.

Friday sniffed the air.

'Always with the sniffing,' said Ian.

'Can you smell that odour?' asked Friday.

'It's disgusting,' said Melanie.

'We've smelled it before,' said Friday. 'It's what Sebastian smelled like on the night of the fire alarm.'

'You're saying he's involved?' asked Ian.

'Minks secrete that spray from an anal scent gland,' said Friday.

'Please!' said Melanie. 'That's way too much information.'

'Sorry,' said Friday. 'Minks spray that scent on people when they're scared. Sebastian must have been handling a mink when it sprayed him. All the counsellors must be in on it. Minks are very aggressive. They give nasty bites and scratches.'

'Which explains why Nadia and Louise have scratched-up arms,' said Ian.

'And why Pedro always wears long sleeves,' said Friday. 'I assumed he had tattoos he wanted to cover. But what if it was actually mink bites?'

'But they're camp counsellors,' said Melanie.

'They must have got jobs at the camp as a cover,' said Friday, 'so they'd have a reason to be out here in the forest,' said Friday. 'The Camp Courage counsellors are all terrible employees. They're missing half the time and they always fall asleep on the job.'

'And it's painfully apparent that Sebastian knows nothing about wilderness survival,' said Ian.

'Do you think Geraldine is in on it?' asked Ian.

'Perhaps that's how she lost her leg?' said Melanie. 'A mink bite?'

'Shhhh!' hissed Friday. 'Get down!'

The three of them bobbed down.

'Why are we hiding?' asked Ian.

'On the far side of the shed,' whispered Friday, 'Pedro just walked in.'

'What are we going to do?' asked Ian.

'We'll have to inform the police,' said Friday.

'Right now we've got to get away from here,' said Ian. 'We can't let them know we've found their operation. The fur trade is a high-stakes trade. They could be dangerous.'

'They already have been,' said Friday. 'Sebastian turned nasty when I announced that we would be heading this way. Now we know why.'

'Let's move,' said Ian as he started to shuffle back towards the cover of the forest. 'We can skirt around the shed and keep going.'

'Wait!' said Friday. 'There could be . . .'

Suddenly Ian stumbled backwards, tripping over a length of string. The string tugged a pulley and a flare shot up into the sky with a loud whistling sound.

'Oh dear,' said Melanie.

At the top of its flight the flare exploded, releasing a bright orange plume of smoke.

'. . . booby traps,' finished Friday.

'I think they know we're here now,' said Melanie.

They could hear Pedro running inside the shed.

'Run!' cried Friday.

Ian grabbed Melanie by the hand and yanked her to her feet. All three of them took off sprinting into the forest.

'What should we do?' asked Ian. 'We can't outrun him.'

'We'll think of something,' said Friday. 'Just keep moving!'

'Maybe he'll sprain his ankle,' said Melanie, ever the optimist.

They broke through the trees, onto the riverbank. The floodwater was still high and moving fast.

'He's got us trapped,' said Ian. 'We can't get away.'

'Yes, we can,' said Friday. 'Look!'

Churning its way upstream, against the heavy flow of water, was a boat. The best kind of boat for three young people trying to escape an illegal fur farmer. A police boat.

Friday, Ian and Melanie started waving and calling out. 'Over here! Help! We need to be rescued!'

The boat altered its course and headed for their spot on the bank.

'I can't believe it!' said Ian. 'We're going to make it out of here.' He put his arms around both girls in celebration.

'He is going to slow down, isn't he?' Melanie was watching the boat and it was gaining speed as it came towards the bank.

'Get out of the way!' cried Friday. She shoved Ian and Melanie aside as the police boat rammed hard onto the bank, the prow narrowly missing their heads.

A policeman vaulted over the side, landing in the shallow water. He looked very familiar.

Ian groaned. 'Not you again.'

It was Sam Fullerton. Ian's kidnapper.

'But it's only a few weeks since we last saw him,' said Melanie. 'He hasn't had time to go to the police academy and qualify as a water police officer.'

'I think we'll find he stole the boat and the uniform,' said Friday.

'Wainscott, you're not getting away from me this time,' cried Fullerton desperately.

'I've got nothing to do with it!' cried Ian. 'Go and harass my dad.'

'I just want what's mine!' pleaded Fullerton.

'Yes, but you keep committing lots of other crimes to try and get it,' said Friday.

'Shut it!' yelled Fullerton. 'I don't have a problem with you. It's the boy I want.'

Fullerton lunged for Ian. And Friday grabbed for Fullerton. They all collapsed in a heap on the ground, writhing as they each tried to get the upper hand.

'Get away from them!'

They all looked up to see Melanie swinging a sock in loops around her head.

Fullerton straightened up. There was clearly something hard and heavy at the bottom of Melanie's sock.

'Don't you try anything,' Fullerton warned.

Melanie took a step forward, still swinging her sock.

Fullerton took a step back to move away. His foot caught on a tree branch and he toppled over backwards, hitting his head on a rock. He lay motionless.

Melanie stood over him as she clutched her sagging sock. 'This rock in the sock tip totally works,' she said.

'Well done, Melanie,' said Friday.

'Come on,' said Ian. 'Let's get out of here before Pedro catches up.' He grabbed the boat by the prow and started pushing it back into the water. 'Jump on, and get the engine started.'

Friday and Melanie scrambled aboard. Melanie sat in the captain's seat and soon had the engine started. Once the boat was safely adrift, Ian jumped on board too.

Melanie was turning the boat into the flow of the river just as Pedro burst out of the trees and ran down the bank and into the water.

'Get back here!' yelled Pedro. He lunged forward and grabbed the side of the boat. Friday picked up an oar and rapped him hard across the back of the knuckles.

'Ow!' yelped Pedro. He let go and was immediately carried away by the current. 'Help!' he cried.

'Just swim to the bank!' called Ian.

'Um, I don't want to be provocative,' said Melanie, 'but isn't there a waterfall near here? The one the Houseboat nearly went over?'

'Oh my goodness, she's right,' said Friday. 'It's about a kilometre downstream.'

'But what about Pedro?' said Melanie.

'We'll let him die,' said Ian.

'We can't do that,' said Friday

'Why must you always insist on doing the right thing?' asked Ian.

'Because it's the right thing,' said Friday.

'Let's pick him up, then,' said Ian. 'But if we all go over the waterfall and die, I'm blaming you.'

They turned and headed over to Pedro.

'Don't let him grab the boat again,' said Friday.

'Then how are we going to save him?' asked Ian.

'Here,' said Friday. She found a rope and threw an end to Pedro. 'Grab hold.' Pedro grabbed the rope and held it tightly. 'Now, let's make for the far shore.'

Half an hour later Friday, Melanie and Ian stumbled into Camp Courage, leading Pedro, who they had tied up with the rope. They were surprised to find the Headmaster being given a guided tour by Geraldine.

'What's going on here?!' demanded the Headmaster. 'Please don't tell me you've kidnapped this man.'

'No, that would be silly,' said Melanie. 'Friday has made a citizen's arrest.'

'What?' demanded the Headmaster.

'This girl has been a troublemaker from the start,' accused Geraldine. 'I've tried to break her spirit, but no amount of potato peeling or latrine digging will do it.'

'They're not sent here to have their spirits broken,'

said the Headmaster. 'They're sent here to learn basic wilderness skills, and get some fresh air.'

'Well, we've had plenty of that,' said Ian.

'You'd better call the police,' said Friday.

'Why?' asked the Headmaster.

'All the counsellors are criminals,' said Friday. 'They've been running a huge illegal mink-farming operation on the other side of the river.'

'And the rest of our group needs to be rescued,' said Melanie.

'Yes, that too,' agreed Friday. 'I can give the rescue services the coordinates. They'll need to treat four children for hypothermia and one man with a sprained ankle and a head injury. Pedro's group have been abandoned somewhere as well, while he snuck down to check on the minks.'

'What's going on?' demanded the Headmaster.

'Camp Courage is a sham,' said Friday.

'I knew it was too good to be true,' said the Headmaster. 'Affordable, convenient and willing to take Highcrest students.'

'It's rubbish!' exclaimed Geraldine. 'Don't believe a word of it.'

'It explains all the strange things that have been happening ever since we arrived,' said Friday. 'The counsellors made up the story about the ghost of Ghost Mountain to keep the students away from the river at night, because that was when they were sneaking over to feed and check on the minks.'

'Which is why the counsellors were always so tired during the day,' said Ian.

'Exactly,' said Friday. 'They wore glow-in-the-dark clothes, like the scrap Drake found, so that if anyone saw them walking along the riverbank they would look like a ghost.'

'But why did Sebastian and Nadia have that argument about cheese?' asked Melanie.

'Because,' said Friday, 'the main food fed to commercially farmed mink is cheese. Expired cheese thrown out by supermarkets and factories.'

The Headmaster turned on Geraldine. 'And you allowed this to go on? Were you involved too?'

'No! It's all lies,' protested Geraldine.

'She wouldn't have known about it,' said Friday. 'The counsellors knew she would never stumble across their operation. With her prosthetic leg, Geraldine would never be able to make it across the rickety old footbridge.'

'You kids wouldn't have found out either if you weren't so nosey,' growled Pedro.

'We weren't being nosey,' said Ian. 'We only stumbled across the shed while we were trying to find help because Sebastian was so incompetent as a wilderness expert he nearly got us all killed.'

'I would have figured it out eventually,' said Friday, 'because there was one thing you couldn't hide – the smell.'

'It's got to do with a deeply unpleasant gland on a mink's bottom,' said Melanie. 'Trust me, you don't want to know the details.'

'But when you applied for the job here you told me you were a former boy scout,' Geraldine accused Pedro. 'You showed me your Queen's Scout certificate.'

Pedro snorted a laugh. 'It took me half an hour to make that on Photoshop. As if you could get anyone with real qualifications to work here with what you pay. We were going to earn ten times what this whole camp is worth with just one shipment.'

'I'm going to kill you!' yelled Geraldine as she launched herself at Pedro, forcing the Headmaster to do the most athletic thing he had done in years. He grabbed hold of Geraldine and restrained her, while Ian pulled Pedro out of the way and Melanie went into the office to call the police.

Chapter 23

In Conclusion

It took a lot of time to sort the mess out. Pedro and Sebastian were easy enough to deal with. Pedro was already captured and Sebastian couldn't run anywhere, so he was still sitting by the riverbank sulking when the police found the rest of the Houseboat team.

The other camp counsellors, Nadia and Louise, tried to make a run for it. Fortunately, their survival skills were every bit as bad as Sebastian's, so the police eventually caught them when they took a rest and sat on an ant hill. They ended up running towards the police, begging to be arrested so they could go to hospital and have the extensive bites to their bottoms taken care of.

Harvey, Wai-Yi, Susan and Patel were taken to hospital in a helicopter. There was nothing wrong with them, but Wai-Yi's mother was an ambassador, so the Chief of Police wanted to make sure that no expense was spared. It was bad enough that a group of children had stumbled across a criminal operation his officers should have discovered. He didn't want an international diplomatic incident on his hands as well.

The Treehouse, Tent and Hole teams all went back to school on the bus. There was a lot of grumbling and complaints. But secretly, most of them were excited to have been supervised by a gang of criminals for four weeks and they couldn't wait to horrify their parents with the news.

Geraldine was taken away. Not to the police station, but to the hospital for a mental-health check. The shock of discovering that she had been unwittingly harbouring a criminal organisation was too much.

She prided herself so much on her discipline that discovering her total failing as a leader had overwhelmed her. She snapped and kept barking at the police officers to "drop and give me twenty".

It turned out that the story of Geraldine breaking her leg and nearly drowning in the river as a child was entirely true. But it hadn't been a counsellor who'd saved her. It had been her father. He'd founded Camp Courage. But he hadn't died in the accident, he'd carried on running the camp for another forty years. When Geraldine inherited the family business, she found it difficult to forgive or forget her terrible accident.

Back at Highcrest, Mrs Marigold was on standby. She had been briefed, and she was personally affronted that her students had been taken someplace where they had not been properly fed. She was whipping up industrial-sized quantities of trifle, banoffee pudding and lasagne to undo the dietary damage that had been done to the students' young growing bodies.

Friday, Ian and Melanie had to stay back at the camp to be interviewed by the police. It was well after dark by the time Friday finished her interview.

She'd had to explain herself several times because the story was so complicated. The police had a hard time following the twists and turns of what had happened. In the end, they'd allowed Melanie to sit in on Friday's interviews to act as a translator. She could tell them what Friday meant when she used unnecessarily long, big words or digressed into pedantic details about science.

Friday was very weary as she trudged out of the mess hall. The camp looked marginally less shabby at night-time. The totally inadequate lighting helped. When she looked up at the sky above, the clouds had finally gone and Friday could see the magnificent spectrum of stars in the Milky Way.

'You know, all the shonkiness of this camp cannot diminish the epic beauty of the night sky out here in the middle of nowhere so far from the light pollution of civilisation,' said Friday.

'I know, it's pretty,' agreed Melanie. 'But frankly, I'd take a little more light pollution for a little less shonkiness.'

'You're just tired,' said Friday.

'I'm always tired,' said Melanie. 'It's just now I've got an actual reason to be.'

'Come on,' said the Headmaster. 'I'm driving you three back myself.'

The Headmaster's BMW was parked off to the side of the courtyard. Ian was already leaning against the side of the car waiting.

'Why?' asked Friday. 'You're not going to do something sinister like drive us all over a cliff because of all the trouble we've caused, are you?

The Headmaster patted Friday on the shoulder. He was proud of Friday, but there was no way he could bring himself to actually say that in words.

'No, I just want to make sure you actually do get back,' said the Headmaster. 'I know what you're like. If I left you to your own devices, you'd probably get diverted trying to solve the Great Train Robbery or find the real identity of Jack the Ripper.'

Friday rubbed her forehead. She was very tired. 'But everyone knows who did the Great Train Robbery,' said Friday. 'Their fingerprints were all over their hideout because they didn't burn it down properly. And anyone with any sense can tell you that Montague John Druitt was Jack the Ripper because all the evidence . . .'

Ian took Friday by the hand. 'Shhh. The Head-master was joking.'

'Oh,' said Friday, with a tired sigh. 'I still miss the social cues for that.'

'I know,' said Ian. 'That's what we love about you.'

'I think I'm going to cry,' said Melanie. 'I love it when exhaustion starts to bring out everyone's true feelings.'

They were all very quiet in the car on the way home. Melanie was asleep as soon as she did her seatbelt up.

Friday and Ian were soon sleeping too. They had been through a difficult four weeks, an arduous two days and way too much walking.

Friday was dreaming about hot baths and kittens purring when suddenly there was a jolt. She woke up and realised that the purring was actually the purr of the car engine and the heat was Ian's body warmth because she was slumped up against him.

'Where are we?' yawned Ian.

'Back at the school,' said the Headmaster.

'Why did we stop so suddenly?' asked Friday.

'Because somebody has parked their motorbike in my parking spot,' said the Headmaster grumpily.

Friday peered out the window. There was a bright red Ducati in front of the car. A leather-clad rider and a pillion passenger got off.

'They look like hitmen,' said Melanie. 'Do you suppose the mink farmers have sent them as a revenge attack?'

The motorcyclists turned and took their helmets off.

Ian gasped. The rider was a stunningly beautiful brunette, and as she shook her hair free she looked like she should be in a shampoo commercial. Next, the passenger took his helmet off, and he was just as good-looking but in a taller, more manly way.

'Who are they?' asked Ian.

'Are they supermodels planning to send their children to our school?' asked Melanie.

'I've never seen them before in my life,' said the Headmaster.

Friday groaned.

'What is it?' asked Ian.

'I know who they are,' said Friday. She opened the door and got out of the car. 'What are you doing here?'

'Friday!' cried the woman. 'So good to see you.' The beautiful brunette leant over and gave Friday a lanky half-hug.

Ian, Melanie and the Headmaster got out of the car too.

Friday turned to them.

'Allow me to introduce you to Quasar and Orion,' said Friday. 'My sister and brother.'

'She's your sister?' asked Ian.

'Yep,' said Friday.

'And he's your brother?' asked Melanie as she openly stared at Orion.

'Hello,' said Orion with a smile.

'And they're physicists?' asked the Headmaster.

'Beautiful people can get PhDs too,' said Friday.

'Yes, but they usually don't bother,' said Ian.

'So what are you two doing here?' asked Friday, turning to her siblings.

'Friday,' said Melanie, 'you know how you like me to let you know when you're being rude. Well, now is one of those times.'

'It's okay,' said Friday. 'It's my family. Emotionally barren bluntness is how we roll.'

'We've got good news,' said Quasar.

'Mum's got you a place at Collège Du Léman,' said Orion.

Now Friday gasped.

Quasar and Orion both smiled smugly.

'What is it?' asked Melanie.

'The best school in Switzerland,' said Friday, 'and arguably, the world. Their science program is second to none.'

'The whole family is in Switzerland now,' said Orion. 'Quasar and I are at ETH Zurich, Quantum is at the University of Bern, Dad and Halley are at the University of Zurich, and Mum is working on the hadron super collider. Mum and Dad want you to join us.'

'They do?' said Friday.

'Of course,' said Quasar.

Friday looked up at Ian. Even when he was tired he was handsome.

'It's a wonderful opportunity,' said Ian. 'Switzerland is beautiful. You could learn to ski.'

'I don't know about that,' said Friday unsurely, 'but I have always wanted to see the super collider.'

Ian smiled a little sadly.

'Excellent,' said Orion, handing Friday a helmet. 'Hop on, we need to head straight to the airport.'

'What?!' exclaimed Friday. 'I can't go now.'

'You have to,' said Quasar. 'Our flight leaves in three hours. And you're starting at your new school tomorrow.'

'Mum had to pull a lot of strings to get you in,' said Orion. 'You've only got one shot at this. You've got to come with us now.'

R. A. Spratt

FRIDAY BARNES
Girl Detective

R. A. Spratt

FRIDAY BARNES
Under Suspicion

R. A. Spratt

FRIDAY BARNES
Big Trouble

R. A. Spratt

FRIDAY BARNES
No Rules

R. A. Spratt

FRIDAY BARNES
The Plot Thickens

R. A. Spratt

FRIDAY BARNES
Danger Ahead

R. A. Spratt

FRIDAY BARNES
Bitter Enemies

R. A. Spratt

FRIDAY BARNES
Never Fear